ACKNOWLEDGEMENT

Thanks to God, Friends, families and my love for encouraging me to write the stories. I am a new writer which makes me a little afraid to say more words. Let me tell you about my story.This story happens in SINLAND city in WAGARD country which is imaginable. This is happening in 1980's. This story is about the effects of negative powers, antichrist and black magic. Steve miller is a leading businessman in sinland city and he has a two children's called Morton and Cassandra. Miller doesn't has the capacity to make the decision by himself and also he is uneducated. He belives Abaddon who can follow the ways of antichrist and worship the devils/satan. And he use black magic, anonymous negative powers to achieve his goal. Miller stands under the shadow of abaddon. Abaddon always stands behind miller to take business and his family decision. This is the reason, Miller bags the criticism that he is selfless thinking person among the sinland peoples. Even Miller ventured into business, he regretted that people criticising about him. Miller wants his children to be good knowledge in education to uplift " Steve Miller Leathers" company against criticism. And he wants his company is one of the best leading company in wagard country. This story contains emotion, fiction, love, horror, betrayal, Investigation. This short story has been narrated as a non-linear format. Please follow the incidents and enjoy the story.

The SINLAND CITY and Dark murder

Present day, Evening 06:45 PM, Sudden thunderstorm and heavy rain, Miller takes off his black full sleeve winter jacket and his grey hand gloves.

Steve Miller and Morton are holding their chairs in the hall. Miller explains the current family situation and business to his son Morton.

Miller clears his throat and takes some water and he starts confessing with his son.

"My boy, You are re-born now. Henceforth, You have to know many things. This is the time to know about our STEVE MILLER LEATHERS company and its development. Before that, you have to achieve in your studies and wipe my criticism from SINLAND city peoples mouth. I am very clear about my decisions and I know what I did to you. It's right for my business and my development."

Morton heard his father's words with irritation and anger. He can't ignore Miller's decision which is final for his family. Morton eye's are looking dark red with tears but he's voiceless now.
He looked into his father's eyes and his mouth while confessing. Miller can understand his feelings but he didn't react.

"Miller, You fucking son of bitch" thinking by his son Morton.

Suddenly, Cassandra enters the hall with a full wet body and shocking face. Her father and Morton was sat at the left side of the door in his home. She turned back and looked at her brother Morton. She got excited and ignored him.

Cassandra's eyes are pale red in color and filled with tears. Her beautiful face was covered with fear and mystery. Miller hasn't seen his daughter before like this.

Miller is able to understand her fears and mystery, He can feel something wrong in his daughter's eyes.He stands up, holds her chin and asks the reason.

" What happened dear?"

She replies with fearness
" Dad, I used to meet Joshua in the hill forest, Same as we have planned for today evening at 6:15 PM. But, we have found Ransley's dead body next to the central tree" says Cassandra with her panic voice.

Morton worries about his sister's words. Miller carry his daughter to murder place. They left Morton at home, But he ready to walk over to murder place.

The SINLAND HILL FOREST, which is a very annoying place in sinland city.

Cassandra holds miller hands and stands backside of her Father, Joshua stands next to Cassandra. Mr. Bran doing his police formalities in murder place. The public also sees Ransley's dead body.

Ransley's mother came to that place with the cop. She saw her son's dead body. Ransley's neck is half open with clotting blood, His mouth is open filling with raining water. She is seeing his neck, then crying continuously with a loud voice and cursing the hidden anonymous powers/Ghosts.

" My dear son, are you alive; are you alive; Can you hear me.
You are the only one i'm having, Please come back to home"
Words of Ransley's mother.

Morton sees this incident far from Ransley's body. He is hearing his mother's words and seeing her tears , Now Morton is speechless.

The public of SINLAND peoples are speaking as this was done by a ghost/satan which is always roaming inside the hill forest. And, One old lady goes near to Mr.Bran and requests.

"Mr. Bran, I'm requesting you, Please seal this hill forest. The ghost is very bad and dangerous to sinland peoples. We know, Everyone in Sinland city peoples knows this is a ghost activity. Our peoples are slaves of ghosts from the 100's of years. Please do something and save us."

Morton hears those lady words too. She crossed over him with the same words. Now, Morton remembers the fight with Ransley which happened a few more days back.

Morton came back to his home and he's thinking about the Ransley's dead body and his Mother's words.

Cassandra and Miller came back to home. While having dinner with her father, She asked about her brother.

" Daddy, Is Morton has all right now, I don't think he will be good for further days. Because he is a killer. He attempted to kill our mother for drugs. Now, our mother is in a coma state. All because of him." Says Cassandra sobbing.

Miller consoles her and he said " Doctor told as it's a brain death, They can't make your mother conscious. Next week I planned to donate your mother organs to the hospital and also a funeral. So, Please accept the reality."

Cassandra went to her bed room with tears.

Cassandra's Love and her paintings:

2 days before murder, Cassandra sharing her bed with Joshua in her house.

Joshua lies his nude body above the Cassandra, Both are covered by blankets. He kisses hardly to her lips and he sees her beautiful eyes.

" Hey baby !, You are fucking awesome and this is a only beautiful eyes, I have seen yet" says Joshua everytime to her lover while fucking.

" This is not a time for cinematic dialogue" is hardly the order of Cassandra.

Both are starts fucking eachother, Joshua loves to see her eyes and face reaction while fucking. She closed her eyes, bit her own lips, and took her paint brush from next to the table and grabbed it in her hands tightly. And she enjoys the painful feelings of love.

Cassandra and Joshua are madly in love with each other. She loves each and every activity of Joshua, Both are doing their higher studies in the same class. Joshua always used to speak positive words and kind heart to people like her mother Claudia. So, Cassandra likes him very much and both are planning to marry after their studies.

Joshua and Cassandra usually meet and make love in " Central tree" Which is inside of Hill forest. The " Central tree" is not a common name of that place. This is the private name of identification for their meeting area.

After sometime, Cassandra placed her chin in Joshua's chest. Her tears are fed down to Joshua's chest.He can feel some tears from her eyes.

" What happened Cassandra ?"

" I'm thinking about my family situation. Suddenly my mom Claudia went unconscious. My brother Morton is in prison. My father always respects Abaddon words but not me. I don't want to live in this home. I will take all my paintings and come with you. Let's marry each other. I want to live with you" Says Cassandra.

Joshua rubs her hairs and hears the words of Cassandra. He wanted to console her and started to ask about her room paintings.

Cassandra has the ability to paint the human feelings as real. Her art will show the feelings of objects or humans. Now she's started explaining about the paintings. Joshua asking about her brother's picture.

" I don't want to picture his feelings. Of course I'm not even trying" said Cassandra.

Joshua noticed her paintings in the wardrobe. It's so anonymous and not understandable. He asked about those paintings.

" I can feel like that whenever I see Abaddon, which was un-explained." Says Cassandra with her low and panic voice.

Joshua saw that painting, And he requested to paint their love. She grab that same paint brush and remembering her painful sex than she started painting about their love in her painting board.After complete the painting, Joshua saw that painting and wondered. He said love you to her and kisses her lips. But Cassandra not complete that painting. She had felt something incomplete in that painting.

Joshua : " Why didn't your father use any influence to release the Morton?"

Cassandra : " Dad Planned to take him out at next 2 days, But I don't want to speak with him"

Joshua : " Don't judge Morton from this incident, I know he's addicted to drugs. But i don't think .."

Cassandra : " Stop! Don't speak about him"

"Sorry, dear! But just think before you act" says Joshua.

After sometime, Both are planning to meet after 2 days in the " central tree" at hill forest.Joshua left from her home.

Cassandra lying in her bed and thinking about her mother.

Miller's announcement:

The next day of murder,

Miller planned to provide compensation to Ransley's mother as per Steve Miller Leather's company policy, Who is alone and poor now. So, he announced satisfactory money and proper shelter to Ransley's mother in the media, which is the breaking news in SINLAND city.

" This announcement is for Ransley's mother. This is the feisty death in SINLAND city, Ransley is an intellectual guy, Because of his educational and researching activity our sinland is more popular. But he is no more now. This is an unequal loss of SINLAND city. I want to help Ransley's family. Our STEVE MILLER LEATHERS company will provide lifetime needful money and shelter to Ransley's mother. Probably Ransley was killed by a ghost or stranger. I hope our cop Mr.Bran will find the mystery shortly" announcement of Miller in the media.

Bran appreciates Miller's announcement through the telephone and the public is happy with Miller activity.After the announcement, Miller wants to see Abaddon and to take his blessings.

STEVE MILLER is a leading growing businessman in SINLAND city, He has a wealth property and passion towards his dream to be the number one steel transporter in WAGARD country. SINLAND is the city where the people believed the supernatural powers, black magic and other anonymous powers which really exist over there.They have a single police station with some efficient manpower. Even sinland people are also having criticism about Steve's business improvement. They were believing like, "Steve is improving his business by using black magic powers and also with the help of Abaddon". Ofcourse, that is partially true.

After this media announcement, Miller criticism has partially faded out from peoples mouth. Which is really happy for Miller.

Miller doesn't have any educational knowledge and self making decision capacity. So,He is always owned the criticism of uneducated and selfless thinking. Whatever he achieved in business,even he is extremely worried about that criticism and Miller is always believing in astrology and other similar stuff. Miller's decision is not only the wishes of him but also Abaddon.

STEVE MILLER wants his children to be very knowledgeable in education and also in social business. He wants to carry forward this company responsibilities to his children Morton and cassandra. This wish not only to take over the business and also to stop the criticism of STEVE MILLER LEATHERS. Miller thought, *" Our next generation of STEVE MILLER LEATHERS should be carried by top rated educational people in WAGARD Country and it must be our children"* like he decides

Morton's Life:

Few more months back of murder day,

Morton is not interested in studying and he used to take drugs regularly. Morton and Cassandra are studying in the same school and same class. Both have 2 years difference in age. Because of poor studies of Morton, The school management decided to do a redo for Morton in his 9th standard. Now both are in the same class and pursuing their higher schooling studies.

Morton is 20 years old and Cassandra is 18 years old. Steve Miller thinks this is the perfect age to build their childerns for business.But they have no interest in taking over Steve Miller Leathers. Morton wants to enjoy life with his girlfriend called Aariana. Who is working as stenographer in STEVE MILLER LEATHERS.

There are a lot of complaints from schools and the public about Morton's activities, Which really affects Miller's mind. But Cassandra is obedient and silent with a kind heart and beautiful too.

One Friday, Morton took the drugs and came to class. Morton's friends complained about Ransley to him. The complaint is , " Ransley having the crush with his sister Cassandra, He is trying to impress her" like that. Ransley is a well defined and educated top rated guy in his school and his class too.

After school, Ransley will use hill forest road to go home, Which is a shortcut to his home. Morton waits over there for Ransley. While entering the hill forest. Morton called Ransley and asked about his love.

" Do you have a crush on Cassandra, Is this true ?" asked morton.

Ransley replies with his kind voice, " Yes, Morton that's true. But..."

" You fucking piece of shit, I will break your teeth" says morton and he started to beat Ransley in hill forest road. Ransley isn't able to refuse him. Morton punched Ransley's face, His nose and mouth started bleeding. Morton's friends came and separated them.

Ransley left from there with heavy bleeding of his nose and mouth.

" Hey, bastard ! If I heard the same news again , You would not be alive. I will cut your neck and kill you in the same place" warned by Morton with his loud voice.

Cassandra heard this news from her friends and she went to Ransley's home

Inside Ransley's home, He is with his mother. His mother is doing first aid for his bleeding.She invited Cassandra to come in.

Ransley's mother went to the kitchen to make coffee, Cassandra hold her chair and sits opposite of Ransley.

" Sorry, Ransley ! I know this is unfair and stupid thing by Morton. And I know about you too, This is fake news" said Cassandra.

Immediately, Ransley replies " No Cassandra, I love you ! I am impressed by your paintings, I love you whenever you encourage my studies and I love your kindness".

"But Ransley, I am in a relationship with Joshua. He is my everything" said Cassandra.

"I know Cassandra, So I didn't disturbed you. Because of this incident , I'm in the situation to tell you. I won't disturb you with my love, Iam always respect your feelings" says Ransley.

Ransley shows his own romantic love poems to Cassandra.She is really impressed and said thankful to Ransley for his love and friendship. Cassandra likes particularly the last line of this poem.

He wrote,

" My love doesn't want to hurt you, But it gives endless support to you…."

Cassandra said " Ransley, I am sorry to hurt you. Thanks to understanding my feelings better than my brother, I'm leaving here with better feelings, Bye.." and she left from his home.

The heavy rain with lightning in SINLAND city.Cassandra came to her home with a wet body and angry with her brother Morton. She went to Morton's room and started arguing with him. Morton gets angry because of his sister's words. So, He slaps her and pushes her away from his room and locks his door.Cassandra told everything to her mother Claudia and she is crying in her mother's lap.

The Abaddon's place:

The next day of Murder,

After the announcement of Miller compensation to Ransley's mother. Miller wants to meet Abaddon and take his blessings. So, he went to Abaddon's place.

Abaddon, **" The personification of evil"**. A tall body with black full sleeve winter jacket, No one hasn't seen his eyes yet, Which is always covered with black glasses.He used to carry his powerful long 6 feet wooden stick like snake in structure in it's top with his hands.

He is a living ghost, who worships the satan/devil in everyday life and follows the way of antichrist. He is having good relationships with miller and his business also.

The SINLAND peoples have the belief of ghost and anonymous powers. Abaddon was doing exorcism to sinland city peoples by using his devil powers, who was affected by black magic and other similar stuff. So, In this case Sinland city people always believe him. They don't care about his way of worship and others.

Aboaddon is the backbone of Miller's ideas and his activities, Miller doesn't have the capacity to make plans and execute properly without Abaddon. Abaddon usually will go to Miller home with him to make his family decisions and business confessions.

Miller went to Abaddon's dark place. His place is full of paintings of antichrist images and devils. The walls and boards are filled with anonymous quotes. Lot's of mirrors but it's not reflecting our images. It's very scary and anonymous to everyone but not Miller.

Abaddon in his dark room, He realizes the miller arrival and he is ready to come out from his room.

Abaddon coming outside from his room. His body shadow is placed on the wall like a beast. Miller stands under his shadow and he smiles while seeing Abaddon's enlarged white devil face.

Abaddon turned his face to Miller.

He raises his magical stick towards miller.

And he said, " Everything is going well. Just make Morton a well educated person and show this sinland city people to wipe your criticism. Now everyone is speaking about your compensation for Ransley's death, Which is a positive publicity for our company. Just do it properly according to our plan."

" I am always thankful to you, I need your blessings at all times," says Miller.

" Miller, this is not enough to make our people talk about your positivity so long. Use this death and do some hidden help to Ransley's family. This silent hidden help to make your character high and good in the sinland people's heart." says Abaddon.

Miller : " But, How other people have come to know my silent help to Ransley's family ?"

Abaddon excited his query and smile,

" How your inability came to be known by our sinland people, Have you told anyone about your knowledge? So, This is also the same way, " says Abaddon.

Miller will not refuse his words, So he decided to do some extra compensation to Ransley's family.Miller is ready to move from Abaddon's place and he's is keep moving with his blessings.Miller reaches the exit gate of Abaddon's place, Suddenly he heard the Abaddon's voice.

Miller turned over back. Abaddon's stands behind him. He was shocked and out two steps backwards.

" Make your hidden help from the hands of Morton" Said by Abaddon.

Miller agreed to his words without any objection and left from his place.

Abaddon is standing over there and he is thinking lonely about something else.

Miller crossed over the outside area of the hill forest region. He saw Mr.Bran over there.
Bran is going to searching the clues in murder place. Meanwhile he met Miller and he wants to speak about Miller compensation.

"Hi Bran, Thanks for giving me the phone call in the morning, I'm really happy with your appreciation," said Miller.

Bran : " No Mr.Miller, This is an unexpected announcement from you. Because the people are criticising about your private and business life, but you are helping them. Now, You are the talk of town in the city."

Miller smiles and leaves the place.

Morton's Love:

Few months back of murder day,

Morton is in a relationship with Aariana. Both are totally different in characters. Morton was impressed by her poems. She is a good writer, From Morton point of view she is a little poet.

Aariana is living with her grandmother. She loves her grandmother like anyone else. Because her parents got divorced and both are married with their loved ones. Finally, she grew up under her grandmother's shadow. She wants to enjoy and live her life for her grandmother.

She is older than Morton. But they don't mind that.

If Morton is present in his father's office room, She is ready to come out with him. This relationship was known by his father Miller, But he is not showing up.

In Aariana's home. Her grandmother went out. Mortons and Aariana doing sex with love in her bed. Aariana is above Morton's body and she bite his lips and chest. Morton moans and he push her down forcefully, He started to do fuck. Aariana lick his lips and moans loudly, While fucking she asks morton.

Aariana with moans, " Morton, do you like me ?"

Morton : " Do you want to show my love to you now!"

Aariana feels the fucking pain and asks, " Morton, just keep doing this love continuously but not drugs, Please stop that."

Morton gets irritated suddenly, He wakes up from her body and sits adjacent to her in bed with an angry face. She felt shocked and asked him the reason.

Aariana : " What happened ? Why did you stop this."

Morton : " I have already told you, Don't give these fucking advices. I don't like this from anyone. I have rights and I know what I'm doing."

Aariana : " No Morton!That's bad to our relationship and your family too. Your father is feeling sad because of your activity."

Morton : " Yeah! He is my shit father, I know how to handle him. This is the last time I'm warning you. If you keep doing this, let us break up."

Aariana with angry : " Morton, This is our life, I'm a mature girl. Just listen to my words, If you keep doing this attitude and drugs. How can we survive in future and you are unfit to run your father's company. Do you want to make his dream fail?"

Morton heard her words and wore his clothings. He got too angry and grabbed her hairs in his hands.

Morton : " How did you know about my father's dream ? I haven't told you about that before. Tell me the truth now."

Aariana felt pain and requested him to take off his hands from her, But he couldn't. Finally Aaraina reveals the truth.

Miller threatened Aariana, as **" I hired you not only for a stenographer position, You have to make love with my boy Morton, for changing his character and make him a good drug free person, If not or you reveal this outside I may have a chance to kill your grandmother"** . Because of her grandmother, Aariana accepts these words and makes a love with morton. Once she realised the love of morton , she fell in love with him.Even Though she was not able to reveal miller words to morton. Because of her grandmother's life.

After knowing all these knots of his father. Morton is getting angry at his father and Aariana. He decides like both are using him for their selfishness. So, he's feeling bad and breaking up with Aariana. He slapped Aariana and he left her house.

Heavy rain with thunderstorm in evening time, Morton enters into his Father's office with a wet body.

Miller checks official files and sees Morton's face. He can feel something went wrong.

He asked everything to his father about what Aariana told him. Miller accepts, and he delivers his points and wishes to Morton.

Morton with tears and angry : " Dad, are you use Aariana to change my fucking character?"

Miller shocked and replied : " Morton, What you are speaking, This is not the way to speak with your father. Go home this is not a private place to speak."

Morton : " I'm not asking about private things, This is also your business too. Just answer my question, are you use Aariana to change my fucking character?"

Morton drinks water and says: " Yes, Morton! Your character is wrong now, Which affects my business and our family. I told you many times but you are not ready to change. I want to hand over this company to a top grade educated person to wipe my criticism but it should be my children. I don't want to give this full company property to Cassandra and her husband. You need to rule this with sharing partner of Cassandra"

Morton : "Any other wishes"

Miller : " Sorry, I don't have another way. So, I used Aariana. But you have to get a top grade in education, I need to show your grade to sinland people, After you and Cassandra have to learn our company tricks and shares then you both have to take over our company."

Heavy thunderstorm.

Morton : " I am going to quit my education and I will not take care of this fucking company anymore, Bye. "

Morton entered his home and ran to his room. Cassandra is sitting in the hall and having bread. She hears Morton's room door lock sound loudly but she doesn't respond.

Claudia and Cassandra hear breaking sounds from Morton's room. Claudia calling Morton's and requesting him to open the doors.

Claudia knocks Morton's room door and asks : " Morton! What happened, Why you are breaking the objects. Please open the door."

Morton : " Don't ask anything to me, You are all selfish, You are all using me for your selfishness. Just go away and leave me alone".

Claudia felt sad and came back to hall. Cassandra seeing her mom's tears and she went to Morton's room. She was going to knock on the door but she didn't. Because she hasn't seen her brother's tears before. She wants to leave him alone for some time.

Cassandra comes back to the hall and sits nearby her mother and says, " He will get alright soon, don't worry mom." She wipes her mother tears.

Claudia is a normal housewife and she has beautiful positive words at all times with her childerns. She respects their children's feelings and she is very obedient to Mr.Steve Miller also. She was married to Miller at her age 18. As per miller perspective, Claudia is a kind hearted housewife with her obedient words and good mother for their children. She doesn't have any rights to take any decision in the Miller family.

The rain had stopped at night 9.00 PM, The entire house was silent, Cassandra and Claudia's were sitting in their hall and waiting for miller.Cassandra requested her mother to ask about this incident to her father.

Cassandra : " Mom, I think something happened between Morton and daddy. Can you please ask about this incident to daddy."

Claudia : " I can't !. How can I raise the question with miller".

Cassandra : " Please mom ! else we couldn't come to know the reason and we can't rectify this problem".

Claudia : " I want to discuss with Morton."

Claudia knocks on Morton's room door. He opened with his red eyes and tears.She was shocked and didn't show up. She enters into his room and sees the breaking objects.Claudia grabbed his hand and asked him to sit on bed.

Claudia : " What are the objects you broke ? Morton."

Morton : " All are gifts from father and Aariana."

Claudia : "What happened, Are you broke up with her?."

Morton with tears: " No mom ! Both of them broke me. They used me for their selfishness."

Cassandra hears the all words of Morton from nearby his room door step.She felt sad and wanted to know what exactly happened to her brother.This is the first time, Cassandra wants to paint her brother's feelings on her board. But she didn't.

Claudia : " Everything will get normal, Just come for dinner and sleep well".

Morton : " I'm planning to quit my education and leave this city".

Claudia is shocked and asks : " No Morton! That's a bad decision, tell me what happened to you? I will ask Miller and recover everything for you".

Morton explains everything to his mother with tears and red eyes. Cassandra and Claudia have been shocked by Morton's words. Cassandra put her hands on her brother's shoulder and she left from his room with sadness.

Claudia : " This is unfair, Definitely I will ask Miller about this. But, don't quit an education. Please change your decision."

Morton : " I want to be alone. Please give me sometime."

Claudia : " Ok Morton ! Sleep well , Don't think about these things and hurt yourself."

Claudia clears his room and she removes the broken things from the floor. Morton didn't sleep, He sits on his bed and waits for his mother to move from his room to take drugs. After cleaning everything, Claudia moves from his room.

Immediately, Morton ran near the door and locked his room and he took drugs from his bag. He used to take the drug through injection, After that his eyes went up and he went into unconsciousness. He fed down to his bed.

Night time, After 11.30 PM,

Miller enters into his house hall,

Miller : " Cassandra! aren't you sleeping ?"

Cassandra : " No dad, I didn't"

Miller : " Why ?"

Cassandra : " Can you make yourself fresh and let us have dinner. "

Miller : " Do you know, What's the time now. why haven't you had your dinner yet?. Claudia what happened to both of you."

Claudia : " Nothing, I will prepare to serve now. Just ready for dinner."

Miller went to his room and he was ready to do a bath. While showering, He is having a thought about Morton. He is thinking *" Maybe Morton has told everything to them or May not be".*

Before going to hall, Miller wants to confirm with Morton.

He knocks the Morton room door slowly. But, He couldn't respond.

Morton stepped down the stairs slowly and thought of Morton. Cassandra noticed his father and asked him to come fast for dinner.

Cassandra : " Dad, Come fast ! I need to sleep."

In dining table.

Morton sits opposite of Cassandra and Claudia.

All of these plates are filled with breads and fruits. Claudia has some fear to ask about Morton's incident to Miller. Because, She never asks questions to miller and made any decisions before in family.

Claudia : " Miller, Why was Morton so sad today ?."

Cassandra : " Mom !, tell him fully."

Claudia clears her throat and says " Yes Miller, I haven't seen him like this before. He broke everything in his room. He is ready to quit his education. All because of you and your plan with Aariana."

Miller : " I don't want to answer your questions. This is a business thing."

Cassandra : " Dad , You had played with Morton's feelings. Why are you not worrying about that?."

Miller : " Cassandra ! Just go to your bed. Don't make me angry."

Cassandra : " I don't go, Without your answers."

Miller seeing Claudia's face, He got angry and he asked Claudia to come to his room. Miller incompletes his dinner and goes to his room.

Inside the room both are shouting at each other.Cassandra gets sad and she goes to her bed room with sadness.

Inside the room,

Miller : " Claudia, this is the first time you are questioning me. I hope this is the last also."

Claudia : " Miller, I have one more question ? . I know this is not the plan for you. You don't have the capability to think like this. This is Abaddon's plan."

After hearing the same criticism from his wife's mouth. Miller got too angry and he slapped his wife and grabbed her hair into his hands. And pull her into him.

Miller : " If you speak another word, I will kill you."

The backend plane of Abaddon,

Miller has a criticism in public as , " *He is always dependent with others, He uses Abaddon's black magic for his business growth, He doesn't have a decision making and planning capacity*" like that. So, Abaddon tells Miller to recruit the local poor peoples for jobs in SINLAND city and also Abaddon builds the idea to Miller for Morton's character change which is very important to our future business career and also to avoid STEVE MILLER LEATHERS critics. So, Abaddon and Miller both decide to make Morton and Cassandra as top grades in studies. But their self life planning does not allow other people's thoughts in their minds. So, Later Abaddon planned and told Miller to select a beautiful and sexy poor girl to avoid criticism and threatened her to make a love with Morton and change his way of thinking. Abaddon says, " **The soul is the master of the brain, Love has a power to influence the other person's soul**". And Abaddon has an alternative plan to change Morton's life but Miller rejects that, he is not ready for that. So, As per Abaddon's words, he recruits Aariana for staging the planning in Morton's life. Abaddon moves the Aariana through Miller's hand.

Next day of Morton's incident,

Now, Miller worries about Morton, He is completely addicted to drugs and he completely hates his father and his business. Miller fears about Morton activities, He is not ready to give the entire company responsibilities to Cassandra. He doesn't want to take over this company by another person like the husband of Cassandra or relatives of claudia. Aariana wants to quit her job. But Abaddon instructs Miller as "don't leave Aariana, Otherwise she has a chance to pieceoff about our life planning to the public". So, Miller doesn't want to leave Aariana from his office and still she is under Miller and abaddon control.

Except for Miller, The entire family knows that Aabadon uses Miller's inability and he earns money.

But Aabadon already knews that, this a stupid plan which is not use to change the

Morton's mind. But this plan is to influence Miller to ready for Abaddon's alternative plan, Which Miller rejects already.

Author to reader : **" Will see later about the alternate plan of Abaddon :-)".**
Miller rejects the alternative plan because he is afraid of that action of plan.Now he has no other way. Because, Abaddon injects the thought to Miller about the words of the outside world as, he is a Brainless person, always dependent on him like that. Now Miller wants to break that criticism from the outside world. Miller has the only way, Morton has to take over the company in future with the partner of his sister Cassandra.

The dark day,

Cassandra has a doubt with her father about Morton's incident. She is having doubt with Abaddon as, "Whether this is her father's plan or Abaddon" .She knows , *" If abaddon means, there is something behind this plan for his benefits".* But she doesn't know what exactly that is.

Cassandra wants to speak with Joshua, Both are meeting in their lovely place called "The Central tree" Which is present inside the hill forest.Cassandra told everything to Joshua. He decides to take a meeting with Aariana for some clear ideas.

Cassandra and Joshua wait for Aariana on the way to her home.

Morton went out from his home to buy drugs.

They enquire Aariana about Morton's incident. While returning Morton to home,He saw everything far from the road.He got angry, he took the knife from his pants and went towards Aariana. Joshua noticed Morton and his knife. He rescues Aariana and he is telling everything to Morton.

Anyway Morton knows everything already ,The same things are revealed to Joshua and Cassandra. Nothing new to Morton, He is getting too angry and he leaves from there. Aariana also left, Joshua and Cassandra are getting confused and they are not able to find the main motive of Abaddon.

This meeting with Aariana makes Morton cry. He took too much drugs and went home.

Morton crossed over the hall, He found one body lying on the floor, He cleared his eyes and noticed, This is his mom Claudia. She lay on the floor without breath and conscious.

Morton fell down floors of shock and slowly went near his mom. She is speechless. He tries to drag his mother into his lap. Because of too much drugs, He drop his body into the floor. So,

Her back head is hitted on floor.Morton also went unconscious and fed down on the floor near his mother.

The Exam Time :

After 2 days of Murder,

Morton wanted to speak with his sister Cassandra. So, one fine morning Morton went to his sister's room and sat near by cassandra. She ignored Morton.

Cassandra says, " Don't try to speak with me Morton !. Because of you, Our mother is under coma. She is not conscious. Doctors also said as this is a brain dead. Next week They are going to plan the funeral and our mother's organs will be donated to the hospital by our father."

Morton left from her bed room.

Morton went to his father's office. Miller introduces each and every important department and explains the working procedure to Morton. Ofcourse, Morton will not take over the company from today even though Miller introduces everything eagerly.

Finally, They came to the production department which is very close to Miller's office room and next to Aariana's place. She looked at him, Miller noticed her and carried him to his office room.

Aariana looked at Morton inside the office room through the window glasses.

Miller and Morton's are confessing about something seriously. Aariana felt wrong, She wanted to hear the conversation. She went inside the room suddenly with some files. That time, she heard the words from Miller are , " Your studies are very important now, Just focus on them".

Miller stops his speech and turns over his face towards Aariana.

Miller : " What happened Aariana ?."

Aariana : " Sir, This is the verification files for upcoming shoe's and Winter Jacket projects. Client needs your self attestation."

Miller : " Keep it on the table and make one Letter Of Acceptance for the same project."

Aariana : " Ok sir."

 She looks at Morton's eye and she leaves the room.

Miller explains about upcoming projects, and latest profitable clients to Morton. And he picturized the process of Shoe's production, Belts, Bags and remaining similar products.

Morton listens to everything carefully.

After the explanation, Again they started confessing about something.Ariana noticed the behaviour of Morton. He kicked the wall and shouted to his father. She enters the inside room with LOA.

Miller : " What now ?."

Aariana : " Letter of Acceptance".

Aariana left from that room, Miller carried Morton out from his company. He takes him to Ransley's home to do the hidden help, Which was the plan of Abaddon for positive publicity.

Morton enters Ransley's home. His face is turned into sadness and his eyes start to leak the tears.

Ransley's mother welcomes Miller and Morton. Both are sitting inside the Ransley's room.

Morton sees Ransley's room, He is seeing the kite which is hanging on the left side of the wall, He is seeing the table , Where Ransley was used to write the poems about Cassandra. Morton opens the Ransley's poem book, He reads all the poems which were written for his sister Cassandra. He noticed Cassandra's last favourite line.

" My love doesn't want to hurt you, But it gives endless support to you...."

Ransley's mother notices his activities and calls him.

Ransley's mother : " Dear boy !."

Morton with his silent voice : " Tell me, aunty !. "

Ransley's Mother : " Are you the guy who beat my son on the hill forest road ?"

Morton turned over backside and wiped his tears,

Morton : "Yes aunty ! This is the hand that broke your son's nose and mouth. But I'm sorry for that."

Ransley's mother : " My son forgives you on the same day. So, I also didn't take that seriously. I'm really happy about your arrival here, If Ransley is here he will also be happy about your arrival."

Miller started to talk to Ransley's mother.

Miller : " My son and daughter are the friends of your son, Being their father I need to do some extra help to you. You have to accept that."

Ransley's mother : " Already you announced too much money and your company is ready to take off me till my death, then why did you do this."

Miller : " I know about Ransley, He is a very intelligent and unique guy in SINLAND city. I feel good to provide this extra money to you. So, Please accept this."

Morton touched Ransley's mother's hand and placed the money.

Morton : " Please accept this, I'm also having the age of your son".

Immediately Ransley's mother accepted the compensation and said heartfelt thanks to Miller and Morton.Both are left from Ransley's home.

Morton reached his home, Miller dropped him into his home and he went to the office. Morton wants to speak with Cassandra and console her.

He went to her bed room and sat next to her.

Morton says, " That day, I came back home. Mother is on the floor, Maybe she unexpectedly fell and her back head hit the floor. I tried to wake her up.Because of my drug influence I can't do anything. Forgive me. But I haven't tried to kill our mother"

" I won't take the drugs anymore. I hate that, Please trust me. And Iam preparing for our upcoming final exams. This is the wish of our mother. I have changed myself for our mother. You also have to study well and get good marks in the final exam."

Cassandra looks at her brother's face and she cries , She was lying her face on Morton's shoulder.

He touches her face and wipes her tears.

Cassandra said , " I don't want to be here. I want to marry Joshua. I have to move on''

Morton takes off his hands from her chin and moves from her bed room. Cassandra called Morton and said, " Please accept Aariana's love.She really loves you".

Morton left from that place without answering.

After the week of Murder, Claudia's funeral day,

One Wednesday,

Abaddon and Miller came together to the hospital. Abaddon has been waiting in the car. Miller went to the chief doctor room to discuss organ donation.

Chief doctor asks Miller to take his chair, Doctor takes off his stethoscope and he starts confessing with him.

Doctor : " Miller ! You are doing great things. The donation of organs is not normal, You are the motivation of good manners for sinland peoples."

Miller adjust his chair and sits comfortable.Then,

" I want to live my wife in the world through another's body. Normally, she's having habits to help others. Even my wife's soul also will get happy because of my decision." Says Miller and drinks the water.

Doctor : " Mr. Miller ! I'm happy with your words. Then what's your next plan for the funeral. Are you taking her body now."

Miller : " Yeah doc!, What about your organ separation formalities."

Doctor : " We have seperated her organs at today morning. So, you just do basic formalities and take her body."

Miller : " And ! I want to do one more thing."

Doctor : " Tell me Mr.Miller."

Miller : " I want to donate my entire body organs now, You can take all parts of body organs after my death."

Doctor excites and says : " Mr. Miller, You are the Man. I really hats off to you, With your permission, I need to announce this news to the entire Sinland city people for their involvement."

Miller : " I agreed for goodness. And thanks for accepting my proposal."

Miller is doing the formalities for his organ donation and He is ready to take his wife's body for funeral.

Morton and Cassandra have arrived at the funeral place and are waiting for their mother's body. Abaddon and Miller are following the ambulance which is going to the funeral place.

" What about organ donation of your body?" asks Abaddon.

Miller : " Yeah ! I have completed the formalities."

Abaddon : " When hospital management will announce to the media about your donation."

Miller : " Don't know ! Maybe later today."

Abaddon : " No, ask them to wait for someday. I will instruct you after that , You tell them to announce in the media."

Miller : " Ok ! Chief doctor also came for the funeral for gratitude. She is inside the ambulance, I will inform them in the funeral place."

Abaddon is the master plan for organ donation. After Claudia's brain death, Miller confesses with Abaddon in his dark place and Miller agrees to donate his organs and Claudia's organs also for his company publicity and wipes his criticism also, But this was planned before the murder incident in hill forest. Now, Abaddon perfectly plans to release this announcement to the public and is waiting for correct timing.

Already Miller is having some positive talk about his help to Ransley's family. So, this announcement made him a gentleman and good human being in front of Sinland people.

In Funeral place,

Claudia's dead body is ready to be buried into earth. Abaddon doing the religious formality. Morton is standing near Cassandra. He holds her hands tightly. She's in tears and looking at her mother's body. Miller is standing on the opposite side and near Abaddon.

Morton and Cassandra , dropped their flowers on their mother's body during the last minute of the funeral. Rain starts in Sinland city,

After the funeral, Abaddon leaves for that place. Miller informs the doctors about the organ donate announcement. He stops that announcement temporarily.

Miller : " Doctor !This is not the right time to inform the public about my organ donation. I'm really sad about this funeral. I will let you know the perfect time."

Doctor : " Ok. Mr. Miller, It's your wish."

Everyone has left from the funeral place.

Miller called Morton to the hall and instructed him to get a high score in the final exam. Morton smiles and he studies continuously. He helped Cassandra also for the exam preparation. She realizes Morton changes after he is released from prison and she is really happy about Morton's good activity. So, She loves to speak and shares her feelings with Morton. Both have done their exams well. Cassandra says about her painting skills to her brother. Cassandra rooms are filled by her paintings. Morton really loves her painting skills.

Exam results came. Morton is the first grade in SINLAND city, All popular media and people are speaking about Miller's struggles to recover Morton from drug habits and appreciating Morton for his unbelievable performance. The SINLAND people spoke positively about Miller company activities, his hidden help and His struggles faced for Morton's life. Miller is very happy about Morton's activity. Cassandra felt happy and shared his feelings to Joshua.

Miller wants to speak with Morton,

 Miller went to his home, knocking on Morton's room door with a glass of scotch. Morton opens the door. But, he was not ready to let him in.

Miller with drinks : " My dear boy, I want to say thanks to you.The bitches of sinland peoples were criticising me like, " I am unfit to run the company, Because I don't have the ability to make decisions and I don't have the educational knowledge". See now, the future of STEVE MILLER LEATHERS is under control of the top rated person. Now, my criticism also fades out from their word of mouth. You have to thank Abaddon, Without him you didn't hit this score." **He drinks again.Morton hears his words patiently.**

Claudia's death :

Before some days of Murder,

The dark day,

Cassandra wants to speak with Joshua to discuss Morton's incident, Both are meeting in their lovely place called "The Central tree" Cassandra told everything to Joshua. He decides to take a meeting with Aariana for some clear ideas.

Cassandra and Joshua wait for Aariana on the way to her home.

Morton went out from his home to buy drugs.

Here, Miller is ready to execute his alternative plan of Abaddon. Miller wants to discuss this plan with his wife Claudia.So, Miller carries Abaddon to his home, Abaddon waits outside of his home. Miller went inside and held his chair in the hall.

Miller calls : " Claudia"

Claudia came to the hall. Miller drags another chair near by him and asks Claudia to sit.

Miller : " I want to discuss Morton and my criticism, I think you aware of about my criticism of Sinland people, and.."

Claudia with her sad voice : "Stop Miller! … I don't want to speak about him anymore. I am worrying about his activities. Now, he is totally addicted to drugs. This all happens because of you and Abaddon.Please don't trust him."

Miller : " Yes, because of Morton activity. I am also worrying, I made the wrong plan. I want to make him clean to wipe my criticism."

Claudia hears his words without seeing his face. She looks at the fish tanks , Fighter fish is searching it's food.Miller continued his speech.

" I have the plan to wipe our business criticism and make Morton clean"

She continuously looked at that fighter fish. Which is hungry.

Cassandra and Joshua enquire Aariana about Morton's incident. While returning Morton to home,He saw everything far from the road.He got angry, he took the knife from his pants and went towards Aariana. Joshua noticed Morton and his knife. He rescues Aariana.

Joshua : " Morton ! just wait, This is not the mistake of Aariana. This is an emotional threat by your father Miller."

Cassandra : " Morton, maybe Abaddon also is involved in this. Please think and act. We have to know Abaddon's exact plan."

Morton drops his knife down and speaks to Cassandra and Joshua.

Morton : " Cassandra I know about your relationship with Joshua. I got angry, But I know Joshua's character. He really takes care of you. I am really happy about your love. But, I loved Ariana more than him."

Morton turns his face to Joshua.

" If Cassandra did something to you for the same reason, are you happy for that activity or what will you do ? . Maybe you forgive her. But I am not like you. My father , Abaddon, and Aaraiana all used me for their selfishness. I can't bear that. Moreover I don't even know what happened around me." Morton says emotionally.

Joshua and Cassandra stand silently.

Abaddon waiting for Miller confirmation outside of his home.

Miller started explaining about the alternative plan to his wife.Rain started with a thunderstorm.

" I have to wipe my criticism and make everything clear. So, I need to do some alternative plan to make this shit clean," Says Morton.

Claudia stands up from her chair to feed the food to that fish, Morton holds her hands and asks her to sit on the chair.and he continues…

" Abaddon is waiting outside, For your confirmation" says Morton.

Claudia turned her face to Morton and asked, " Why that devil is here." with her angry face.

Rain continued, He didn't bother about her words and started explaining an alternative plan to her.

Claudia is shocked and her tears are touching her chins.She got angry and shouted.

Claudia with her loud voice : "You fucking bitch ! This is a criminal thing. He is my son, How can I allow this fucking plan to him. No, Just go away."

Miller : " Claudia, My business is more important than other emotions, You have co-operate this. Aren't you happy about my business improvement and Morton's improvement."

Claudia : " You brainless idiot, If you execute this plan ! He is not my son Morton, He wasn't born from my worm. Please don't put this type of black magic into my son's body. I'm requesting you to drop the plan."

Miller : " No Claudia, My apologies to you. I haven't discussed this with you. I made a mistake. Anyway I'm going to execute this plan. I don't have any other way to stop my criticism."

Claudia with her thundering voice : " If you ready to do this, I will inform the cops now. I will carry my children into my cousin's home. I won't stay here anymore. I will talk about this plan to the Sinland media. The entire city will criticise you. Be ready for that."

Miller got angry and he slapped her, He held her neck into the wall and said, " I will execute this plan with the help of Abaddon's power. If you try to interrupt, I will kill you."

On road with heavy rain,

Aariana cries and said to morton,

Aariana : " You are not understanding my feelings, But I can understand yours, I'm leaving from here."

Aaraina left from that place with tears.

Joshua : " Morton, You have to continue the education again, Your sister and mother is worrying about your activities. At Least you have to think about your mother."

Cassandra : " Morton, I didn't ask anything from you. Please don't make our mother sad. Please continue the education and be free from these drugs."

Morton turned back to the way,

Joshua : " Morton, Where are you going.?"

Morton : " To buy drugs, This is not enough today. You all made me sad."

Cassandra gets angry by his words and leaves from that place, Joshua also left with Cassandra.

Miller came out from his home angry. and explain everything to Abaddon.

Miller : " No, Claudia is not ready for that plan. I'm getting angry at his words. Do you have any alternate plans?"

Heavy thunderstorm,

Abaddon turns his face to the direction of thunder and asks miller.

"Miller, do you want a wife for making decisions or do you want a wife to accept your decisions?" asks Abaddon.

Miller came in front of Abaddon and chose the second option.

" Miller, you want Morton's with an intelligent and helpful or drug addicted useless son" asks Abaddon.

Miller chose the first one.

Abaddon turns back and he walks towards Miller's home.Miller walks behind him. The lightning also happens behind the hill forest heavily, Which reflects backside of Abaddon.

Abaddon enters Miller's hall.

Claudia sat on her chair, She was shocked by the arrival of Abaddon with her husband Miller.

Claudia : " You shit devil , Just get out of my home." Shouting her panic voice.

Abaddon raised his magical stick towards Claudia and started using his magical quotes.After raising his stick towards her, She stood ideal, speechless. Miller sees everything and gets shocked, But he was not trying to help her.

Thunderstorm continuing,

Claudia walks towards Abaddon, and stands at the edge of that magical stick. Abaddon pressing that stick on the head of Claudia. He is trying to control her soul and make her unconscious.

The rain stops, Claudia fall on the floor,

" Claudia's soul was separated from her body. Now, It's under the control of me, Which is inside my ring. Just leave her body here. Everything will happen positively to us trust me" Says Abaddon.

 He already did the same to lots of people for his selfishness.
Abaddon sees that fish tank, That fighter fish is swimming fastly, He asks Miller to take the fish food. And finally, Abaddon feeds the food to that fish and Both are left from that place.

Morton came back home with a wet body and full drugs. He is literally unconscious and he is thinking about that road conversation with Aariana. He is getting a confusing mind about the knots of Abaddon and also a floating mind.

He came inside the hall, and crossed the dining table, He saw some big object on the floor with his blurring vision He clears his eyes and sees that place.

His mother was lying on the floor speechless, He was trying to reach that place, But he also fell down on the table. The glasses and water flasks fall on the floor and break. He went there and held her mother's chin and tried to wake her up. He touched that floor water and placed it into her eyes. Claudia is speechless now.

He checks the heartbeat of Claudia, Which is normal. Now, he wants to lift her up and take her to hospital. Because of Morton's drug, he also went into an unconscious state and finally both are fed down on the floor.

Morton opens his eyes, He is in hospital under the control of sinland police. Bran arrested Morton for taking drugs and attacking his mother.He lifted his head up and searched Cassandra to explain the reality.

Cassandra, Joshua and Miller were standing outside the room. Cassandra sees Morton's consciousness through a glass door. But she doesn't want to speak with him.

Cassandra went to her Mother's room and she held her mother's hand and cried.

Bran's Investigation :

At Murder day,

Evening 6:00 PM, Cassandra waiting for Joshua in "Central tree". They have planned to meet at 6:15 PM today.

Cassandra felt some bad smell and eagles over her head. So, She moves from there and walks inside the forest. She can see some stranger's body which is on the earth. She goes near that and is shocked and two steps back. That's Ransley, His head was cut into half, Eagles are eating his neck flesh.She started to run away from there.

She can see Joshua far from her. She shouted his name and ran towards him. Joshua also panic about her voice and coming near to Cassandra, He holds her shoulder and asks,

" What happened ? Cassandra, Why your chin is read and voices are so panicked."

Cassandra : " I saw Ransley's dead body, His neck was cut into half."

Joshua is shocked and says : " Wait, Let's see."

 Cassandra : " No Joshua, Will inform the police."

Joshua : " Ok, But wait."

Heavy thundering and started raining,

Joshua walks slowly towards Ransley's body.Cassandra comes behind him.Joshua sees Ransley's face and he is shocked.

Joshua : " Let me go and inform the police. You just go home."

Joshua running to the police station from hill forest and Cassandra running to her home to inform about this murder to her father Miller.

Heavy raining, Evening 6:45 PM.

Her father Miller with her brother Morton, Both are confessing about their family and business. Morton sits on the opposite side of Miller.

Cassandra enters her home and she goes to the hall.

Cassandra's eyes are pale red in color and filled with tears. Her beautiful face was covered with fear and mystery. Miller hasn't seen his daughter before like this.

Miller is able to understand her fears and mystery, He can feel something wrong in his daughter's eyes.He stands up, holds her chin and asks the reason.

" What happened dear?"

She replies with fearness

" Dad, I used to meet Joshua in the hill forest, Same as we have planned for today evening at 6:15 PM. But, we have found Ransley's dead body next to the central tree" says Cassandra with her panic voice.

Miller gives some water to Cassandra and asks her to sit in a chair.

Cassandra ask her father to carry the Murder place, Morton stands adjacent side of Cassandra.He felt worrying about her sister voice. Miller is ready to go with his daughter and he asks his son Morton to stay at home.

Joshua went to police station,

Mr.Bran doing the formalities to closing the Morton's drug dealiing and attumpt murder case. He lifted that file into the shelf.

Joshua enters the police station with a wet body and red eyes with tears.

Mr.Bran saw Joshua's fear in his eyes and he asked.

" Why are you coming like this? Who are you?."

Joshua introduced himself and says,

" Sir, I used to meet my lover inside the hill forest. Same we have planned today. But, we saw Ransley's dead body next to our place. His neck was cut into half. He is my classmate and friend too. Please come," with his panic voice and fearful face.

Both are ready to go hill forest,

Murder place, Heavy rain.

Miller came to murder place with his daughter Cassandra.

Joshua stands near Bran, Bran makes the analysis of Ransley's body and he's doing the formalities for autopsy. Joshua saw the arrival of Cassandra with her father. He went there and asked Cassandra.

Joshua : " Why did you come here again?."

Cassandra with tears : " Ransley is my friend."

Bran came near to Miller and says,

" This is the second time we have met today." Miller smiles.

Bran : " If you don't mind, I just ask general questions to your daughter Cassandra."

Miller shows the way to Cassandra through his hands.

Bran : " Are you the person to see Ransley dead body at first."

Cassandra : " Yes. But, I don't know how long it will be here."

Bran : " Was he in class today."

Cassandra :" Yes"

Bran : " When it is over, I mean your class."

Cassandra : " 03:00 PM"

Bran : " So, Might be he have to reach his home within 4.30 PM or 5:00PM right?"

Cassandra is silent and holds Joshua's hand.

Ransley's mother came with cops and she's crying of her son's death in front of Cassandra and Ransley's body.

She saw her son's dead body. Ransley's neck is half open with clotting blood, His mouth is open filling with raining water. She is seeing his neck, then crying continuously with a loud voice and cursing the hidden anonymous powers/Ghosts.

" My dear son, are you alive; are you alive; Can you hear me.You are the only one i'm having, Please come back to home".Words of Ransley's mother.

Bran gets emotional and he walks to do other official formalities.

The public of SINLAND peoples are speaking as this was done by a ghost/satan which is always roaming inside the hill forest. And, One old lady goes near to Mr.Bran and requests.

"Mr.Bran, I'm requesting you, Please seal this hill forest. The ghost is very bad and dangerous to sinland peoples. We know, Everyone in Sinland city peoples knows this is a ghost activity. Our peoples are slaves of ghosts from the 100's of years. Please do something and save us."

Bran hears that public voices and he thinks about this murder, Whether is this way done by killer or by any anonymous power. He turned over his head and he saw Morton over there. Morton stands far from the Ransley's body and he is seeing that old lady face and he is ready to step away from there. Bran is looking at Morton while he moves from there.

In Midnight, Bran seals the Hill forest and announces it as a restricted area.

Next day of Murder,

Bran in discuss with Forensic department,

Bran examines the reports of Forensic and he is doing general discussion with them.

Bran : " Can you to say whether this is a murder or something what sinland peoples says."

Forensic officer : " No Bran, We have not said anything like that. We will examine the clues and details of crime and make a report for cops."

Bran : " Ok !Then tell me about your investigations."

Forensic Officer : " Have you noticed the victim's neck?"

Bran : "Yes, Victim neck has been cut into half."

Forensic Officer : " Right !. But the neck veins in the victim's body were cut parallel and deeply, which makes heavy blood loss. Maybe the killer uses the long sword to cut his neck."

Bran : " mmm. But If he uses the sword means , His neck will be seperate from his body. But see the corner of his neck. " Bran shows the dead body's picture", Here, the fleshes are irregular in shape. So, maybe there is a chance someone will try to ripper his neck."

Forensic Officer : " Correct Bran, Killer cut his neck into half . But, In your document you mentioned eagles presence are around the victim's body. Maybe Eagles are trying to eat his flesh, So, His corner neck flesh was coming outside."

Bran documented every word of the forensic department.

" Mr.Bran, You have to notice the main thing, If the kill was using the sword means, Victim's body will lose lots of blood. But, As per our crew document, there is no blood flow clues in murder place ." Says the Forensic Officer.

Bran documented this important point and asked.

" May have a chance like, Someone killed the victim in another place and placed the body in a hill forest."

Forensic Officer : " Yes, Maybe. But you have found them and one more thing the victim's front tooth was broken, But as per our examines it's was not happened at murder day, It was happened few days back. Because the broken teeth were healed, so we confirmed it happened a few more days back ."

Bran : " Well, Thank you officer for your support. Let's see the killer is a human or devil".

Bran came to his room and started reading his documents and analyzing Ransley's body picture.

Now, Bran is getting the news about Miller's compensation to Ransley's mother.He is getting excited and calling Miller through the telephone.

Miller : " Yes, This is Miller."

Bran : " Hai, Mr. Miller ! Just now I heard the news about your hot announcement. Which is very useful to Ransley's family."

Miller : " Yeah ! Thank you. I know about Ransley. He is an intelligent and well knowledged person in sinland city, My childrens are the classmates of him. Cassandra worried about his death and also she worried about his mother. Because of Cassandra I was announced this compensation."

Bran : " Nice to speak to you Miller, How about Morton and Claudia."

Miller : " After being released from prison, Morton didn't use drugs. But we are worrying about Claudia. Morton also worries about her and he is going to continue his studies soon for her mother. Which is very happy for me and my family."

Bran : " Oh! Miller, you are giving lots of surprise announcements for me. Okay TakeCare of your family. Bye.."
Bran wants to start investigating Ransley's manner from his class friends and faculties.

Ransley's Class,

Bran went to Ransley's classroom with the permission of management. Cassandra and Joshua are not available in the classroom. Morton also not available in class.

Bran investigates each and every student separately,

Bran's common question to students, " Tell me about Ransley's behaviour and studies."

All students are told the same answer, " Sir, He is intelligent in studies and other educational activities. He is having a good friendship with others, even the faculties."

Bran documented everything,

Morton's friend : " Sir, Once Ransley had the fight with Morton.But It's not inside the campus.So, no one knows about this"

Bran : " Why?"

Morton's friend : " Ransley loves Morton's sister Cassandra. But she didn't. This news was known by Morton. So, He beaten Ransley and broke his teeth at the entrance of hill forest."

Bran : " Why does Ransley use the hill forest way?"

Morton's friend : " Sir, That's the shortest way to reach Ransley home. So, he used it."

Bran : " Thank you for your valuable information."

Bran left from that place.

Bran investigates the faculties of Ransley, Everyone saying the common answers like students but no one knows about the fight incident of Morton and Ransley.

Bran wants to see that hill forest entry where Morton and Ransley had fought with each other. And he wants to check the blood flow clues of Ransley's body and also he wants to check the distance to Ransley home from the hill forest. So, Bran is ready to go to the hill forest now.

Bran reached the entrance of the hill forest.He is seeing the place where Morton and Ransley had fought each other.

That time, Miller crossed over the outside area of the hill forest region after met Abaddon in his dark place. Abaddon advised Miller to make hidden help to Ransley's family by the hands of Morton to wipe his son's older bad names and Miller positive publicity.

Bran met Miller and started confessing to each other about Miller's announcement.

Miller: "Hi Bran, Thanks for giving me the phone call in the morning, I'm really happy with your appreciation,"

Bran : " No Mr.Miller, This is an unexpected announcement from you. Because the people are criticising about your private and business life, but you are helping them. Now, You are the talk of town in the city."

Miller smiles and leaves the place.

Bran wants to investigate Cassandra and Morton without the knowledge of Miller. If Miller knows he will rescue them by using his influence and also he doesn't want to spoil his good names because of his investigation.

Bran went inside to the hill forest to search the clues, He couldn't find any blood flow track of Ransley.

Few days later,

Bran gets the news like, " Miller provides extra compensation to Ransley's mother, Which is not announced to the public and media". He is getting doubt of Miller and his activities. He's started enquire indirectly to sinland peoples about this hidden help.

Sinland peoples are appreciating Miller activity and his business development in a positive manner. 90% of Miller criticisms have faded out from sinland people's mouth.If his son Morton got the good grade in the final exam and took over the company, Miller is the king in sinland.The final exam will come within a few days.

After a week of murder, One wednesday.

Bran wants to visit Ransley's home to get the more details about Ransley and about Miller's hidden help.

This is Claudia's funeral day, The miller families are going to funeral. Bran went to investigate Ransley's mother.

Rain started in sinland city,

Bran enters Ransley 's home. His mother welcomes him and asks him to sit inside the Ransley's room.Bran seeing the pictures of walls , Kites and Poems was written by Ransley.

Bran : " Sorry to disturb you again, I'm the person to investiges Ransley murder."

Ransley's mother : " Mr. Bran, This is not a murder I know, This was done by anonymous power or devil which is live in hill forest."

Bran : " How do you tell like that?"

Ransley's mother : " Our sinland people are slaves for that from the past 100 years. We don't have a single church in our city, I told Ransley many times , avoid to use the way of hill forest."

Bran : " Yes, I know, But the normal roadway and hill forest way are the same distance to your home. I was examines the way at the next day of murder. Then why does Ransley use that way?."

Ransley's mother : " Yes, he loves the daughter of Miller, Cassandra. But she didn't. Cassandra and Joshua were sometimes met inside the hill forest. Ransley wants to see Cassandra. He doesn't know the dates and times of their meeting. So normally he used the hill forest way."

Bran : " How did you know these details?"

Ransley's mother : " He told everything about his love on the day he fought with Morton. After our discussion, Cassandra came to our home to see Ransley as a friend."

Bran thinks " Oh ! It's interesting".

Rain continuous,

"Cassandra likes Ransley's particular line in his poem. That too Ransley told me." Said Ransley's mother and she showed that line to Bran.

Bran seeing that line,

" My love doesn't want to hurt you, But it gives endless support to you…." Bran likes it.

He documented everything and continuous his question,

Bran : " Was Miller providing you any extra compensation for Ransley's death, Because, outside sinland peoples are spreading rumors like that."

Ransley's mother : " Yes ! Miller and his son Morton both came to home and provided extra money and some help to me. These are all excluded from his press announcement. I really respect him. He is having a good human heart."

Bran : "Then, you are confirming this death happened because of the devil."

Ransley's mother : " Yes, I have confirmed. Few years back, Abaddon controls all devils which are all inside the city and he locks inside the hill forest. Maybe this is rumors of city peoples or true. But, Hill forest is a mysterious place for all."

Bran ensured about hidden help and documented. Finally he left from that place.

Now, Bran wants to meet Abaddon, to get a clear idea about ghosts and devils. But, he cannot meet him directly. So, he planned to take the help of Miller to arrange the meetings with Abaddon.

The Alternative plan:

Few days before murder,

Miller failed to change the character of his son Morton. Because of Miller activity Morton affects a lot and he is totally addicted to drugs which hurts and gives negative names to miller business. So, as per Abaddon's instruction Miller is ready for an alternative plan called " **SOUL TRANSFER"** which means, They have planned to murder a person who is best in education and well in manner, Then they will seprate his soul from victim's body by the help of Abaddon. Here, Miller is ready to do the same for Morton, After that, Abaddon will lock Morton's soul and transfer the victim's soul to Morton's body. This is the plan that Abaddon instructs Miller.

Now Miller is also ready for a Soul Transfer, He wants to discuss this to Claudia, But Claudia was not ready to transfer the soul.While discussing with Claudia,

 She said, " If anonymous souls will rule your company means it's not like our son, The credits are not for our family. This criticism is worse than what people are throwing to us now".

 She requested Miller to drop this idea.

Miller said , " I want my son with capable knowledge to carry our company and I don't want to carry my criticism in future and I don't care about his soul and other stuff ".

Finally, Abaddon separates Claudia's soul from her body and locks into his ring. But he can't manage the other person's soul into his ring for a long time.So, He used to lock the anonymous souls to his mirror which is in Abaddon's dark place. After he locks the soul into the mirror, it won't reflect the objects. There are lots of mirrors like this in Abaddon's place. So, Finally Abaddon locks Claudia's soul into his mirror.

Morton has been caught by Bran for drug dealing and attempt murder case.

Abaddon and Miller are discussing the plan of soul transfer in his place.

Abaddon : " Miller don't use your influence to release Morton from prison now."

Miller : " No Abaddon, These incidents spoiled my business names more, I'm feeling worse."

Abaddon : " This is the perfect timing to search the fit person for your company and your family."

Miller : " How can we do soul transfer now. Because Morton is in prison, We need his body to execute the plan."

Abaddon : " You take him out from the prison on our plan executing day, I will let you know."
One fine day,

Miller has found one research thesis file in his table. That is the thesis overview of Ransley. Ransley needs money to continue this thesis. But, This thesis idea is helpful and profitable for Miller business. Miller already provides many scholarships to educated people in sinland city. So, Ransley plans to take the help with Miller to complete this research.

Miller started analysis of Ransley, He was impressed by his education performance and activities especially the research idea. So, Finally Miller chose Ransley to transfer the soul and he is ready to discuss this with Abaddon.

Miller went to Abaddon's place and started planning to murder Ransley.

Abaddon : " Don't give any appointment to meet him, the Ransley family should not know about the thesis discussion between you and him."

Miller : " I haven't met him yet, But I knew him. He is the perfect person for my business. If Morton is like him, My business career will grow up and my criticism also will fade out from sinland peoples mouth."

Abaddon : " Now, You can try to release Morton from prison by using your influence and confirm the date."

Miller : " Okay, I'm leaving."

Now, Miller is planning to release Morton from prison. After some days, By using his influence MIller arranged to release Morton within the next 3 days.

Miller enters his hall, Cassandra sits in a chair and she is worried about her mother Claudia and Morton's situation. Miller starts to console her.

Miller : " Dear, don't worry ! Everything will be okay within the next 3 days. I have arranged to release morton."

Cassandra : " I am worrying about my mom, Why Morton did like that?."

Miller : " Whatever happened it just happened, We can't change. I hope Morton will change after his release."

Two days before murder,

Joshua came to Cassandra's home to console her. Miller is not at home. Cassandra is in her bedroom. He went there. She's getting ready in front of the mirror. He is standing behind her and placing his chin to her chin and hugging her backwards, His breathing air is touching her lips. Both were facing the mirror and started talking.

Cassandra with her lovely and romantic voice : " What are you doing in my room?"

Joshua : " I just came to see my angel."

Cassandra : " Have you seen her."

Joshua : " Yes, But not fully."

Cassandra turns her face suddenly, Both are facing each other's eyes and slowly Cassandra starts kissing his lips and both are kissing each other roughly and went to her bed.

After the romantic sex,

Cassandra placed her chin on Joshua's chest. Her tears are fed down to Joshua's chest.He can feel some tears from her eyes.

" What happened Cassandra ?"

" I'm thinking about my family situation. Suddenly my mom Claudia went unconscious. My brother Morton is in prison. My father always respects Abaddon words but not me. I don't want to live in this home. I will take all my paintings and come with you. Let's marry each other. I want to live with you" Says Cassandra.

Joshua : " Why didn't your father use any influence to release the Morton?"

Cassandra : " Dad Planned to take him out at next 2 days, But I don't want to speak with him"

Joshua : " Don't judge Morton from this incident, I know he's addicted to drugs. But i don't think .."

Cassandra : " Stop! Don't speak about him"

"Sorry, dear! But just think before you act" says Joshua.
Then, both are planning to meet after two days in "Central tree".

The Murder day,

Abaddon and Miller plan to kidnap Ransley and Kill. This response was given to Miller by Abaddon. Miller is ready to kidnap according to Abaddon 's plan. And that same day Miller plans to take Morton out of prison. Ransley used forest road to go home.

Morton is supposed to release at evening 5'0 Clock. Ransley class will end at 3'0 Clock. Abaddon and Miller have planned to Kidnap Ransley at 3.30. Miller waits for Ransley behind the tree with Grey color full covered Mask and Grey color hand gloves. He wears a full sleeve black winter jacket, With black leather shoes. Miller is ready to kidnap Ransley. Miller hears the sound of Ransley, He covered his face by mask.

Once Ransley crossed him, Miller walked behind him slowly. Thunderstorm started with heavy wind. Maybe rain will come in the next 4 to 5 hours. Immediately Miller covers Ransley's face with his kerchief which was soaked in chloroform. Ransley went unconscious, Miller lifted him and he took him into Abaddon's place.

Miller locks Ransley in Abaddon's place, Anyway he is not conscious.Now, Abaddon and Miller get ready to pick Morton from the prison.

At 5.00 PM, Morton was released from the prison, he came out and entered Miller's car. Abaddon sits in the backseat of his car. He covered Morton's face with the same handkerchief. Morton also went unconscious.

The entire sinland city in cloudy climate with thunderstorm,

Miller places Ransley and Morton on table, Which is in front of Abaddon. The first time Abaddon removes his shirt in front of Miller, but not eye glasses. Miller is shocked, because Abaddon's bodies are full of scars and anonymous quotes, The quotes represent him as an antichrist and he worships the devils.

Abaddon took his wooden stick and he started the process of separating Morton's soul from his body and locking it into his mirror. He started using his magical devil quotes, Morton's body is 2 feet in the air, then Morton soul came out from his body. His body has fallen down now.Abaddon controls his soul by using his magical stick and continuing his quotes. Now Morton's soul has been locked into the mirror. Abaddon kept his magical stick down and he took his sword and He looked miller eyes and started using the same quotes.Suddenly, Miller lost his self control and Abaddon gave this sword to Miller. He instructed him to cut half the neck of Ransley.

Miller cuts Ransley's neck by sword. Immediately, Abaddon inserts his face into Ransley's half neck and sucks all the flowing blood of Ransley. Ransley was dead. Both are killed Ransley ruthlessly.

Ransley's soul is free from his body and it's crying in front of Miller and Abaddon. It asks the reason for his murder. Miller regained his control and he saw the neck of Ransley and he's afraid and fell down. Abaddon started to answer for Ransley's soul. Ransley's soul is worrying about his dream and his mother.

Miller words:

``` Now, You are in abaddon control. We will make your dream come true through Morton's body,Your mother will be safe.Steve Miller Leathers will give money for your loss and we will take care of your mother's entire life by the policy of Steve miller's Leathers. If you are required, We will give extra money to your mother. And you can continue your study and research through Morton. My Requirement is ``You have to be a good knowledgeable person in all the crafts and You have to learn our company tricks and take care of our company at your age 27".``

Abaddon Words :

" Ransley, If you try to do stupid things. Your mother's soul will be in next to my mirror. Your Mother's life in your action. As openly, From this minute your soul is my slave".

After 10 seconds silence of Ransley, He is accepting the words of Miller and abaddon.

Morton's soul is crying inside the mirror. Claudia's soul is next to Morton's mirror.

This process has to complete within 6.0 Clock. So, he started to transfer the soul of Ransley into Morton's empty body. Process completed, Morton woke up and saw Abaddon and Miller face with anger.But He wasn't able to do anything. Miller took Morton and Ransley's body. Miller drops Ransley's body in "THE CENTRAL TREE" with the help of Morton. Morton sees that body for a minute. Miller asks Morton to get in the car. Both are reached home.

Miller clears his throat and takes some water and he starts confessing with his son.

"My boy, You are re-born now. Henceforth, You have to know many things. This is the time to know about our STEVE MILLER LEATHERS company and its development. Before that, you have to achieve in your studies and wipe my criticism from SINLAND city peoples mouth. I am very clear about my decisions and I know what I did to you. It's right for my business and my development."
```

After 2 days,
Ransley's soul wants to speak with Cassandra. Because she is not feeling good, She's thinking about her mother Claudia, who was hospitalized by Abaddon. Ransley soul got all the information about her mother's condition and he got a doubt with Miller. So, Morton went to Miller's office to ask about the reason for Claudia's condition.

Miller hears his question but he doesn't answer him. Aariana also sees the conversation through window glasses and she is disturbing them. Miller takes Morton to show the production process in his company. Again they came to Miller's office room, And Miller explained the true reason for Claudia's condition and he took Morton to Ransley's home to provide extra money (hidden help) through the hand of Morton/Ransley's soul.

The Pre-Plan of Abaddon and Miller:

By using the Ransley death, Abaddon plans to get the positive publicity for Miller's life and his business. Abaddon told everything to miller, to donate the organ of claudia for publicity, Give good fund and settlement to Ransley's mother for wipes the criticism and for attract the sinland people, Inform to Bran about Morton drug free habits for his son criminal clearance, Reveal Claudi's brain death to Ransley soul and asks Morton to console Cassandra for family happiness, Now Morton got a good exam result also and Everything is going well. Steve Miller Leathers company got a positive response from the SINLAND Peoples. He's gained lots of profits in business by using the Ransley research thesis.

Finally, The masterbrain for Miller and his business is Abaddon.

Murder place Incident :

Present day,

Bran wants to investigate Cassandra and Morton without the knowledge of Miller. If Miller knows he will rescue them by using his influence and also he doesn't want to spoil his good names because of his investigation.

Before that, Bran wants to meet Abaddon, to get a clear idea about ghosts and devils. But, he cannot meet him directly. So, he planned to take the help of Miller to arrange the meetings with Abaddon.

Aariana wants to meet Morton and she wishes to congratulate him. She met Morton on the road with fear. But Ransley's soul hasn't any idea about Aariana.

Aariana says, " Morton, I wish to congratulate you, Iam really happy about your activities now and Because of your activity your father's name and your company name are growing well and positive. Post your prison time, This is an unbelievable transformation. You are an angry guy but now you are listening to my words. Thanks for a time."

 Morton keeps silent.

Aariana kisses his lips. Morton pushed her away and avoided her and left from that place. Aariana realised that,Still he didn't forgive her.

Aariana is still in love with Morton. She knows that the complete character of morton. Because at earlier times she tried to change his character. But Morton is not ready to change his character, Even he is ready to break up with Aariana. Now, She's wondering about his changes.Aariana doesn't want to speak about Mortan's change anymore. But she wants to live with him. She's planning to speak with Miller about her feelings, Because everything was started by Miller.

Aaraina enters Miller's office room, and starts speaking about her feelings to him.

Aariana : " Mr. Miller, I still love your son Morton. I won't tell him about our earlier planning. I will promise you."

Miller smiles and replies,

" Aariana, are you joking! already told everything to Morton. So, nothing new to tell him." says Miller.
Aariana : " No Mr.Miller, I don't want to think about our old conversation, I will sacrifice anything for Morton. Please allow me to live with him."

Miller gets irritated by her words and he replies with anger.

" Are you ready to sacrifice your grandmother for Morton?" says Miller.

Aariana got shocked and silent,She looks down with tears then she replied.

" Mr. Miller, I will obey your words and don't hurt my grandmother."

Aaraina left from that place , Miller got angry with her speech. He got irritated and he also left the office.

Miller reached his home, He sat in the hall.

Cassandra also came to the hall, and sat opposite to her father Miller.She wanted to speak about her life with Joshua.Both are having their coffee's.

Cassandra : " Dad, you know me and Joshua in a relationship. We have planned to marry soon. So, I need your permission."

Miller got more irritated, but not shown to her daughter.

Miller : " Cassandra ! You have the right to choose your partner. I am happy with your decision."

Cassandra : " Thank you , dad !"

Miller : " I am not completed yet, You can marry him after you and Morton will take over the company."

Cassandra thinks and reply,

" It's okay ! and I wanna tell you something. I am really happy these days. Morton has changed a lot. He doesn't have drug habits, He got a good score in exams, He loves my painting and also he spends more time with me. Your criticism also faded out from people's mouth. Our business is also developing well because of Morton's idea, which is unbelievable. Our mother's losses change him totally." **says Cassandra.**

Miller : " Gladly, I'm moving out. Bye.."
Miller is going to Abaddon's place. And he's telling everything to Abaddon. He agreed for Cassandra and Joshua marriage but not the love of Aariana. Because, Aariana knows every attitude of Morton. May have a chance to confuse everything.

While Miller discussing about Aariana's love with Abaddon, Bran calls to Miller. He attended the call and put it in the speaker. Bran asks Miller to arrange the meeting with Abaddon.Abaddon hears that and tells Miller to carry Bran to his place. Miller conveyed the same to Bran. So, Finally the meeting was scheduled for the next day.

The next day, Miller carries Bran along with Aariana to Aabadon's place. Everyone is standing around the table of Abaddon. Bran standing in the middle of Miller and Aariana and opposite of abaddon. Miller asking about supernatural powers to Aabadon and slowly he's started the doubts of Ransley's murder.

Bran asks Abaddon, about the ideology of Ransley's death.

Bran : " I don't want to make the conclusion of Ransley's death. Few days back,I was investigating Ransley's mother. She assures that her son's death was caused by ghosts/some anonymous powers. Even sinland peoples also believe the same. Ransley's mother said that, Few years back, you had controlled all devils which are all inside the city and locked inside the hill forest. Is that true?"

Abaddon : " Yes, There are lots of anonymous powers that were ruined in this city, This city was cursed by satan. I controlled all the devils and locked it in the hill forest with the help of my god satan."

Aariana hears the words of Abaddon with fears and excitement.

Bran : " If i am not wrong, You are also the devil right. Because you also follow the same antichrist concepts and worship the devils. I saw your place when I came here. It's full of antichrist quotes in your wall."

Abaddon : " I think you are familiar with the words of " Diamond cuts diamond". I am using this power to control the black magic powers , removing the curse of sinland peoples, and sometimes clearing the cops' doubts about supernatural powers".

Bran : " Okay, then what's your ideology about Ransley's death?"

Aariana fears increases,

Abaddon : " Ransley's mother said true. It was caused by Ghost or any other anonymous power."

Bran is not ready to accept this simple answer. He keeps asking doubts about anonymous powers.

Aariana keeps hearing the confession between Bran and Abaddon. Suddenly she falls down on the floor. Miller tries to wake her up. She wakes up after 2 minutes. Bran doesn't want to make the conclusion by Abaddon. He wants to clarify the doubts of anonymous powers which are spreading over Ransley's death.

Finally, Abaddon asks for the photograph of Ransley's dead body.

Abaddon : " Have you noticed the Ransley's neck, It was ripped in the edges."

Bran : " Yeah, I have noticed, Maybe eagles damage that. But his neck veins are cut parallely, Maybe the killer used a big sword to cut his neck."

Abaddon : " I can't find any blood flow over that place, You can see the tooth marks near the flesh of neck, I can sure .This was done by blood sucking ghosts. Trust me."

Bran was already examining the forensic report. His doubt is about those tooth marks which are mysterious, Now he has some clarity in his mind. But, he is not ready to show that without the proof.

Bran : " How can I trust you, prove it."

Abaddon : " I am able to show you the proof. But, it's dangerous. If you are ready, I will proceed further."

Abaddon seeing bran's face and he ask miller to take them into murder place for showing that ghost infront of bran. Bran accepts that word

Bran documented all words of abaddon and he is ready to go, Miller carry all persons to murder place " The central tree".

Murder place,

All four members are forming a circle and sit in circle formation. Abaddon starts using his magical quotes.

After 10 Minutes,

Bran and Miller can feel some rotten smell.Wind blowing heavily, Thunderstorm started with raining.Suddenly the big central tree is falling down near Aariana.Everyone fears and Aariana falls down and goes unconscious.
Bran tries to wake her up. Aabadon and Miller stand behind Bran, Abaddon continuing his magic words.He asked the help of abaddon.

Thunderstorm continuous,

Suddenly, Aariana wakes up, and bite the Bran's side neck. Her tooth is penetrating his neck slowly. Blood starts flowing out. Abaddon pushes her away with his magical stick.

Now everyone realised , Aariana was occupied by some anonymous power.

Bran is standing besides of Aariana,

she looks Abaddon and said,

" Someone is disturbing me, By using powerful words, I don't want humans to be here. Just go away."

Bran cover his blood with his hand kerchief, and asks question to Aariana with fear,

" Are you killing Ransley?" asks Ransley.

She turns her head towards Bran and said,

" I don't know who that is, If I had tasted someone's blood. I want to suck that." She smiles.

Abaddon use his magical words again, Rain continuous,

" Who's blood who had sucked at last?" asks Abaddon.

She turns to Abaddon and says, " I had tasted one human blood a few months back. which is present at the entrance of hill forest. I waited for that person for a long time. Few days back he came back, I tore his neck and sucked his blood."

Bran remembers the Ransley fight with Morton, Which was happened at the entry of hill forest. That day Ransley had heavy bleeding in his mouth.

Suddenly, she turned her neck towards Bran. And she said,

" Now, I tasted your blood." She laughs loudly, Thundering heavily in the hill forest region.

Everyone gets shocked and Abaddon uses his magic words to save Bran.

Abaddon asked Bran to leave this place.
Bran holds his blood and runs away from that place.

Aariana gets angry and starts shouting loudly. Miller closes his ears.She wants to sucks the Bran's blood. She's trying to move to that place, But she can't. Abaddon controls her and tells Bran to go away from here with his loud thundering voice.

Bran went so far from that place. But he is able to see them.

Aariana laughs, blood starts bleeding from her mouth. She is looking weird and anonymous. Her hair is flying in the air.

Suddenly, she punched the earth. Abaddon and Miller fly away from there, and fell down little bit far from there,

She started running from there,

Abaddon and Miller run behind her. Bran watching everything from so far.

Unexpectedly,

Aariana falls from that hill forest to the crater. Her head was hit on the multiple rocks and it broke. At last Aariana was dead.

Everyone gets shocked, Raining continuously,

Miller and Abaddon come back to the car, Bran is in shock.

Abaddon : " I have already told you about the difficulties of this process. Because of you, Aariana was dead."

Bran : " I am sorry, I can't tell you anything now. Now I can understand the powers of ghosts."

Miller : " Bran, go to the doctor first for the wound in your neck."

Immediately, All of them are leaving from the hill forest.

Joshua having the doubts with Abaddon. Because, He can't believe Morton's character change, His exam results, and Miller's sudden development.

Joshua thinks like, " Maybe Abaddon is using his black magic to change the Morton character and business development, Which is wrong." But he didn't show up to Cassandra. Because she is happy in recent days. He doesn't want to spoil that. He decides to follow Abaddon and Miller.

After this incident, Bran was ready to close the Ransley's murder case file. Aariana is also dead. Now, There is no problem for Abaddon and Miller.Bran getting nightmares while sleeping. He is thinking about the same incident and decided to close the case by using the same reason within a week.

Mastermind :

The previous day, Bran called Miller, While Miller confessed about Aariana and Morton's love to Aabadon. Miller accepted the Bran call and He conveyed the same to Bran what Abaddon told Miller.Abaddon planned to kill Aariana and at the sametime to escape from Bran's investigation. Abaddon used Claudia's soul.

Abaddon makes the slave of Claudia's soul. Which was already in Abaddon mirror control.

Now, Claudia's soul has to act what Abaddon mind instructs to it, Or else, Abaddon will kill permanently the soul of Morton. Claudia's soul doesn't have another option. Before Bran arrives Abaddon makes Claudia's soul a slave of his words.While Bran confesses with Abaddon, Miller starts the magical words to insert Claudia's soul into Aariana's body, Which was already trained by Aabadon to Miller. Abaddon attaracts Bran's entire concentration at their conversation. After Claudia's soul enters Aarian's body, She falls down and others wake her up.

Now Claudi's soul is under control and a slave of Abaddon's words.So, If he instructs to act and speak means, Claudia's soul will speak. Whatever happened in murder place, all are instructed by Abaddon to Claudia's soul. Finally, He instructs it to jump from a hill forest.After Bran moves to his home. Abaddon takes Claudia's and Aarian's souls to his control and locks in his mirror. **Abaddon sits in his chair and thinks lonely and deeply.**

Joshua's Instinct:

Joshua has doubts with Abaddon's activity. So, He decides to follow him.

One fine day, Miller and Abaddon are going by car, Joshua followed them. Both of them are going to Abaddon's place. Joshua followed them and hid behind the tree.

He's watching them. Both are speaking something but he can't guess. But his instinct knows that they are doing something which is wrong. Again Abaddon and Miller were left from that place.Joshua went inside his place. He is seeing everything as weird.He went inside to Abaddon's private room.

Joshua can see more than 15 mirrors in Abaddon's place. But he isn't able to see his face inside the mirror. He got shocked and left from there.

Joshua wants to meet Bran to discuss Abaddon.

After 3 days,

Joshua went to Bran's home and he told about Abaddon and miller. Bran getting his words and he try to convince Joshua and he explained what was really happened in Murder place. But Joshua told as

" Mr.Bran please don't leave this conversation outside. Please make this confidential" **says Joshua.**

Joshua : " Mr. Bran, Please don't close this case. Please start this investigation from Abaddon and Miller point of view."

And also he remembers manythings to Bran.

" Mr. Bran, Just think about Morton's sudden character change, His exam results, Miller business development and Nowadays people having positive words about Miller. These are changed like magic. I think Abaddon's super powers are helping their development." says Joshua.

Bran : " Ok Man, What is the relation between your points and Ransley death."

Joshua : " I don't know sir, But something is there."

But both having no idea about the link between Ransley's death and the rest of the incidents.

After the coffee time,

Bran's linking Morton to Ransley's death and says to joshua about his instinct,

Bran : " Joshua, I think Morton is involved in this murder?"

Joshua : " How ?"

Bran : " Morton was released from prison at the same day of Ransley's murder. I was saw Morton in Murder day evening, He came with his father. But he stands far from the Ransley body and watches everything, And also already both are fighting with each other for Cassandra."

Joshua doesn't know about that fight until Bran reveals.

Joshua : " When ?"

Bran : " Don't you know, Ransley loves Cassandra, But she didn't. I think you and Cassandra are in a relationship right. Was she didn't informed?"

Joshua : "No ." Bran smiles,

Joshua said " bye" and left Bran's home.

Bran decides to start investigating Ransley's death. He wants to enquire about Morton, Cassandra, Miller and Finally Abaddon.

Bran calls Miller to take appointment for a private investigation.

Meanwhile he saw Miller's announcement in the media, " Miller provides compensation to Aariana's grandmother and Steve Miller Leather will take care of her, Because Aariana is the employee of them."

After 10 minutes, Another announcement from hospital of sinland city, " Miller donates his entire body organs to hospital. He is a great inspiration for sinland peoples." Like that.

Miller attends his call and replies,

Miller : " Yes, Bran."

Bran : " I am really excited and shocked by your one by one news in the media. Great Miller."

Miller : " Thank you Bran." and silently he asks, " Are you closed the Ransley's murder file."

Bran : " I called you for that only, I want to investigate Cassandra and Morton finally."

Miller : " What ?"

Bran : " Sorry Miller, But I need to do it. Cassandra, Morton and Ransley are classmates, You knew that, Maybe i will get some extra information from them. I went to their class to investigate their friends, But that day Cassandra and Morton were absent from class. And also, Morton and Ransley having fights with each other for Cassandra. Ransley loves your daughter Cassandra, But she didn't. This was mentioned in my case file. I have to provide justification for that. You also have good names in Sinland peoples. So, I don't want to do this officially, Will make a private meeting in your home."

Miller : " Finally, he gives the date for investigation next week."

Miller knows about that fight, But he doesn't know that was for his daughter Cassandra.

Morton's Play :

Before three days of Joshua meeting with Bran,

Morton came inside the Cassandra bedroom. She's reading a book. Morton asked Cassandra about her love relationship with Joshua.

Morton : " Cassandra, How about your love with Joshua."

Cassandra : " Yeah , It's good. I'm happy these recent days with my family and Joshua."

Morton : " I am happy for you." Morton ready for next question,

Cassandra smiles and closes her book, looking at Morton.

Morton : " Even, I like his character and way of behaviour in class, He is handling everything as very mature and cool. I love that."

Cassandra : " I am also impressed in the same way. Do you know one thing, he is super cool and very patient. He never makes me uncomfortable and angry these lovable days."

Cassandra continues her speech about Joshua to Ransley's soul / Morton, This is the first time her brother asks about her feelings. So, she gets excited and tells everything.

" I was totally depressed and feeling unsafe in your prison days, Because of your activity and our Mother's condition. Joshua is the only person who shares his shoulder for my tears and makes me good. I loved him like anyone else. I want to marry him soon and want to be part of his life." says Cassandra.

Ransley's soul hears the words of Cassandra and gets jealous of Joshua.Because, Ransley already has a crush on Cassandra. But, This is the first time he hears the words about Joshua from Cassandra's mouth.

Morton : " Is our father aware about your love."

Cassandra : " Are you kidding, How many times have we all had dinner in our home with Joshua. He knows everything about my love."

Morton : " Then, What's the next plan, When you have a plan for your marriage?"

Cassandra : " Soon, Already I had discussed with our dad, He agreed but he is not ready to make it now."

Morton : " Why, ?"

Cassandra : " Our father wants us to take over his business. After that, the rest of my dream will happen."

Morton : "Are you interested in that?"

Cassandra : " Of Course not, But he has agreed for marriage. And also he tried more to develop his business. I just want to help you in business. Because, this is a share for both of us. I just said ok for you and daddy."

Morton : " Well ! good ."

Cassandra : " Once I will take the company, My first thing is to avoid Abaddon from our family and business side."

Morton keeps silence and smiles.

Morton : " I want to ask you something, I know Joshua is good in all. How about your sexual life. Is he able to satisfy you? or Just he is satisfying himself in bed. I know you are not virgin now."

Cassandra gets shocked by his words and she cannot speak anything to him. This is a weird and shocking moment for her.

Cassandra : " Morton !What are you speaking?"

Morton : " I mean.."

Cassandra : " Stop! Don't speak more than that."

Morton : " Sex is also essential. Don't you know, You are mature now. Don't overreact for silly things."

Cassandra with her angry : " I am your sister, What the fuck you are talking."

Morton gets angry and says,

Morton : " I am not asking anything wrong. Just keep your emotions with you. Don't shout me."

Cassandra : " Morton, This is the limit, Just get away from my room. I don't want to speak to you anymore. Don't come to my private life."

Morton left the room with anger. Cassandra is still in shock.

Next day,

Cassandra is sick , So Morton didn't go outside. He is taking care of Cassandra. Joshua came to her house to see Cassandra.Morton in the hall, He is thinking about something.

Joshua : " Hi sweety!, What happend?"

Cassandra wakes up from bed and reply

" Nothing, normal fever. Anyway happy to see you Josh."

Joshua sits near Cassandra and he keeps his hand in Cassandra's head and asks, " Are you ok now!."

Cassandra with a little smile: " No! Take me to your home."

Joshua : " I'm ready, Just pack up your paintings and come with me."

Cassandra turned her head to the adjacent side of joshua and said, " I'm also thinking the same."

Joshua felt wrong in Cassandra's words.He turns her head towards him and asks,

" Why what happened?Everything is alright now, Any problem again."

Cassandra : " No nothing, I cannot wait until my father's handover his company to me. I want to live with you soon."

Joshua breathed and came close to Cassandra's face and said, " I know, you have disturbed by something, Soon I will take you to my home."

Morton prepares coffee in the kitchen for Joshua and Cassandra. After that, He came from with 2 coffee cups to his sister's room.And hearing their conversation from the door.

Joshua holds her chin and say,

" Soon, I will take my painting into my home. Just wait for a few days, Now I'm leaving, take care."

Cassandra holds his hands and says, " Am I painting for you?"

Joshua : " Yes."

Cassandra holds his hands very tight and say,

" Then, give me the kiss in my lips." Says Cassandra.

Joshua holds her chin and kisses her lips with heavy breathing. Both are kissing each other's lips deeply. Morton saw that incident , He gets angry and Knocks the door. Cassandra gets away from Joshua's lips and adjusts her dress and sits properly. Joshua sees him and sits in the corner of bed.

Joshua : " Hi Morton, Thanks for the Coffee."

Morton is angry and says, " Gladly."

Joshua drinks the coffee and he says " Bye" to them and leaves from home.

Morton locks the main door in home and comes to Cassandra's room. She sits in the bed , and she doesn't have that coffee. Morton sees that coffee cup and took in his hand, sits near Cassandra and say,

Morton : " Why didn't you have my coffee?."

Cassandra : "I am not feeling well,I don't want that."

Morton touches her chin and forehead to check the temperature of fever. She pushes his hands away from her chin.Morton smiles and he notices the forehead, chin, eyebrows, neck, lips of Cassandra. He goes close to Cassandra and notices her lips which are a little bit bleeding because of Joshua's force kiss.Morton picks her lips in his hands and say,

" I don't want to hurt , I know you are getting pain because of this fucking kiss" and suddenly he licks that blood by his tongue from her lips.

Cassandra is pushed away from bed and her coffee cups are fallen down and broken.

Morton collects the broken cups from the floor with hearing of Cassandra's words.

Cassandra angrily and cry, " Why are you doing like this, you are my brother. Please leave me. I will go with Joshua."

Morton smiles and he's continuously picking the broken cup from the floor.

Cassandra finally, " If you are doing this, I will tell our dad about your activity."

Morton looks up at Cassandra's face and stands up. He smiles and starts moving from that room. then, suddenly he stops walking and say,

" Again, I am telling you I don't want to hurt you." Then he left the room.

Cassandra cries with anger continuously, He cannot tell this incident to any one. And she doesn't want to tell Joshua.

After Joshua meets Bran, He wants to meet Cassandra to discuss about the Ransley's love.

Cassandra sits in the hall and drinks the juice, Morton comes to hall and sits on the opposite side to Cassandra. He is pouring water into his glass and speaks to Cassandra. Cassandra doesn't want to speak to him, She stands up and is ready to move from there.

Morton : "Cassandra sit, I want to speak with. Please hear my words."

Cassandra sits and starts hearing his words.

" I am sorry for what happened before. I was ashamed of my activity. Please forgive me. I want to carry over our mother's words. I have to take over our company and make it more profitable.Please don't tell dad. Otherwise, he will plan something bad. Please Cassandra.." says Morton with tears in her eyes.

Cassandra keeps silent and says, " Okay leave it."

Morton : " Thank you, Cassandra.." Suddenly Joshua enters the hall. Morton gets angry but he doesn't show up. Cassandra welcomes him and sees Morton's face. Morton smiles and takes the chair for Joshua, Then he moves far from there. But he can hear their conversation.

Joshua: " Was Ransley loves you."

Cassandra : " Yes Joshua, But that's an old chapter. Why are you asking about that."
Joshua : "Why didn't you tell me?"

Cassandra : " No, that's not a big deal. Ransley loves me but he never hurts until he dies. You know he is a good human being. I also like him. But I loved you."

Joshua : "Okay relax, I am just asking." He kisses her forehead and he says " bye" to both of them.

Morton hears everything about their conversation, But he doesn't react. He went to Cassandra's room and saw all the paintings on her wall and touched her beds and pillows. He feels her feelings in her bed which makes him more tempt. And , he opens her wardrobe and sees the remaining picture. Some pictures are looking weird and he didn't understand anything. Suddenly, Cassandra came in and asked.

Cassandra with a loud voice: " Morton, What are you doing in my room."

Morton : "Don't mistake me, I am just seeing your pictures, What is this it's so weird."

Cassandra : "I don't want to explain to you, Just get out of my room."

Morton : " Okay, Cool. I have a wish, Can you please paint my feelings."

Cassandra : " No, Without realizing anything I can't."

Morton : " Okay, At least can you paint my picture."

Cassandra agreed finally and asked Morton to sit in the chair. She makes ready to paint Morton. She starts to paint Morton, Ransley's soul sits silently and sees the beauty of Cassandra. He is seeing her cat eyes and slim hips and thighs. He is getting tempted but not showing up.

Always Cassandra starts painting from upside down. So, She starts painting Morton's shoes, Legs, hips, shoulders and all. But he sees Cassandra's beauty, which feels uncomfortable to her. But she also does not show up.

Finally, Cassandra paint his face, She got an illusion that to make a sex with stranger. Suddenly she disturbed and put her paintbrush down.Morton ran near to her and touched her shoulder and asked , " What happened Cassandra?". She takes off his hands and says, " Nothing." You can go and sit. I will complete the painting.

She started to paint his face again. Again she got a illusion that to make a hard sex with Joshua with moaning sound.She's sweating and she stops painting. Morton took some water and gave it to Cassandera. Morton sees her throat while she's drinking the water. Finally, she stops the painting without a head.

Cassandra went to the hall and thought about her illusion.

Miler comes home and sits in the hall. He also wants to speak to Cassandra about Ransley's love. Which was informed by Bran through telephone.

Miller started confessing with Cassandra. But already she is in a bad mood.

Miller: " How is your health dear?"

Cassandra : " Yeah dad, It's good now."

Miller: " Then, why your face is so sad."

Cassandra: "Nothing dad, tell me."

Miller : " Bran called me to discuss Ransley's death.He wants to investigate our family privately."

Cassandra: "Why ? Is he in doubt with our family?"

Miller : " No, He noticed about Ransley's love in her file. He wants to justify that point with your words and Morton also fights with Ransley for you. So, Maybe just a general investigation."

Cassandra: "Okay dad, When he will come."

Miller : " Maybe next week, Then, Why didn't you inform me about Ransley's love."

She got angry because everyone was asking about that. She told everything good about Ransley and she said as, " He doesn't even involve my love relationship with Joshua. He is good dad. Nut Morton misunderstood him and fought with each other. Apart from nothing to say."

Miller : " Okay dear, Leave it. Where is Morton?"

Miller is angry with Ransley's soul for hiding his love with his daughter. So, he wants to speak with Ransley's soul now.Meanwhile, Cassandra called her father and told everything about Morton what he did to her in previous days and also she said about her illusion while painting.Miller gets shocked and goes to Morton's room.

Dealing with soul :

Miller went to Morton's room with anger. Morton sits in his room bed and writes something in his diary. Miller calls him, Morton keeps his diary on the table and welcomes him.

Ransley's Soul : " Tell me, Miller."

Miller hold his neck and push him to wall and say,

" You asshole, You fucking bitch… You cheated me."

Ransley's soul with a smile: " Was Cassandra told you?"

Miller : " You cheated me, Why are you hiding your love?."

Ransley's soul : " I am not selecting you, You selected me. I am not an asshole. You are the fucking cheater and ruthless killer."

Miller : " Your soul is under Abaddon's control, are you forgetting that."

Ransley's soul : " Of Course not, I have obeyed your words, I have helped your business development. You used my fucking reserch idea and making you profit. I will support your future business also. Why can't you sacrifice your daughter for me."

Miller : " You fuck, Your are in Morton's body. Who's her brother?"

Ransley's soul : " But, Feelings is mine. Mr.Miller."

Miller : " No. I can't accept this fucking words. Let's meet Abaddon."

Ransley's Soul : " I expect this word, Because, you are a brainless bitch."

Miller is angry and says : " I will kill your mother. Don't forget."

Immediately, Ransley's soul : " I will take your daughter."

Miller shouted loudly, Cassandra came inside the room, But she thought this fight was because of her blame to Morton and she went to her room.

Finally, Miller takes Morton into Abaddon's place.
Miller explains about Morton's activity to Abaddon. Abaddon gets angry and he starts a conversation with Morton.Miller stands next to Morton.

Abaddon : " What's your demand now, I know your intention is not Cassandra, tell me what do you want?"

Ransley's soul : " WOW ! I wondered, How could you find this?"

Abaddon : " Don't speak unnecessarily, Just tell me."

Ransley's soul : " You both separated me from my mother. You have used my skills , used my ideas and researches and made profits , just think about my mother. If I submit my research to the government, My family will get richer than what you have."

Abaddon : " We have already provided lots of money to your mother. which is more than what you expect."

Ransley's soul : " I need more."

Abaddon : " How much?"

Ransley's soul : "I need 40% shares of Miller's all projects and also upcoming projects too."

Abaddon and Miller get shocked and Miller gets angry.

Miller with his angry voice : " Do you know the value of 40% share."

Ransley's soul : " Yes I know, You have explained everything to me. and I know the value of my research."

Miller keeps silent and asks Abaddon to do something.

Abaddon : "We will give, what you want, But You must not see your mother anymore."

Ransley's soul : " You have to directly share the money to my mother's name with my concern. If you satisfy my demands I will leave Cassandra."

Abaddon goes close to Ransley's soul and says, " This should be your last demand, If anything you plan I will kill your mom and lock your soul in my mirror."

Ransley's soul keeps silent and sees miller.

Miller : " Abaddon, why we have to give money to him. His soul is our slave, do something."

Abaddon : " No, His evilness thought is more dangerous than what you are thinking. May your family will get divided and your business will go down. Just give what he demands."

Miller agrees with anger.

Miller makes an agreement with Ransley's soul and he makes arrangements to do what Ransley's soul demands.

The share transfer to Ransley's mother was taken care of by Abaddon from Miller.

The Unexpected :

Cassandra meets Joshua in his home and he tells about Morton's activity to him. He got angry and consoled her with some lovely words. Both sketches their signature to each other's chests and makes some romantic love.Then, Cassandra came to home.

This is the day Bran has to come home to enquire Morton, Cassandra and Miller. So, Everyone should be home before 2:00 PM. Miller has already informed this investigation to both of them. Cassandra in the kitchen, She prepares the food for lunch to everyone. Miller will come to lunch and he will attend the investigation.

Morton inside his room,

Ransley's soul can't control his evilness, He want to make sex with Cassandra. He imaged about Cassandra schooling days, Cassandra's love with Joshua,Cassandra's sex with Joshua, Cassandra's kisses with Joshua, Cassandra's thighs while she doing painting, Her lips while he licks her blood. This made him to make a rough sex with Cassandra today.

Cassandra is alone at home. Morton went to the kitchen and he's trying to seduce Cassandra with her wrong touch.She's feeling uncomfortable with his touches. So, Cassandra asks Morton to step out of the kitchen. Finally, he decide to make her unconscious and do sex with her.He is taking a iron rod and walking slowly towords behind Cassandra.

Suddenly Miller came inside the home and saw Morton's activity and He called Morton with his loud voice. Suddenly, he dropped an iron rod into the floor. Morton got too angry, because of his disturbance. Morton pulled Cassandra in front of Miller and he tried to hug and kiss her. Miller got angry and used that same rod and hit into his back head. Morton turns over and sees Miller's face. Suddenly Miller cut off his neck.

Cassandra gets shocked, Morton suddenly falls on the floor. Ransley's soul was free from his body and went away.Now, Miller future plans are wasted.Anyway, he wants to cover this murder. He requested Cassandra.

Miller with a fearful face and tears : " Cassandra, please don't tell this incident to anyone. Even Joshua."

Cassandra didn't speak anything, She was in shock and tears. Miller shouted at her and told the same again.

Cassandra : " Dad, our family gets this situation. I can't be happy about what you did?"

Miller : " What, He is your brother, he is trying to fuck you. Do you agree with this?"

Cassandra : " Dad, Please don't tell me that word."

Miller : " I will cover this incident as suicide. Please don't tell anyone. Because, Our business and family names are growing well nowadays. Why do you want to spoil that?"

Cassandra with crying face: " Do it, What you want. I will not tell anyone."

Bran is getting ready to go to the Miller's house for investigation. Meanwhile he got the suicide news of Morton. He's shocked and leaves from his office to Miller's home. Bran sees Morton's body inside his bedroom. His neck is cut off by using a knife, Which is in Morton's hand. Bran has a doubt but he doesn't want to show out.

Miller decided to do the funeral within 2 hours. Bran with Miller and Cassandra, Bran asking permission to Miller to examine his body. But Miller refuses that and he's looking for a further funeral process.

Miller says to Bran, " He has started to use drugs again. I locked him for the last two days. So, He made this decision. If this will leak to sinland people means my hard work for my business and my good names, Cassandra's life everything will go wrong. So, Please don't examine anything and Make it confidential".

Bran accepts his words and leaves from there.

After 2 hours of funeral, Miller went to Abaddon's place. He informed everything to him. Abaddon gets angry and makes a loud voice.

Abaddon : " Do you know, What fuck you did?"

Miller : " He crossed his limits. He tries to seduce my daughter."

Abaddon : " You have to tell me, This is my plan. Iam also involving Ransley's murder, Aariana's death and Claudia's brain death.Without me you are nothing"

Miller with an angry voice : " Abaddon, don't speak too much. You have just planned. I only took risks to do all those things, You are working for me for money. Just keep that your mind"

Abaddon : " You brainless fucking bitch. Just get away from my eyes, Otherwise I will kill you."

Miller got too angry, Because Abaddon also criticized him with the same word. And he left from Abaddon's place.

Abaddon makes a shout with his loud voice, Which makes echo in hill forest.

Bran's investigation got cancelled, But he gets a doubt in Morton's death. He tries to link Ransley's death and Morton's death.

He thinks like, " Maybe Morton is the killer in Ransley's case. After Bran informs Miller about his fight with Ransley, Miller asks about that to Morton. Maybe Morton agrees with his words.Miller kills him to save his good name."

Miller gets sad, His dream is spoiled now. After a few days, Cassandra told her father to marry Joshua. He didn't say anything and he asked for time to think.Miller was not able to reach Abaddon.

Miller went to Abaddon's place also. Bit he's not there.

Cassandra feels alone now.

Bran investigates to Miller:

Cassandra slept at night, She got a dream about his beautiful conversation at exam preparation with Morton. She wakes up and thinks about Morton. She can feel good at the initial times of Morton that means after he is released from prison. She is thinking about his bad activities at recent times. She realizes that attitude and behaviour has totally changed from his previous days.

She went to Morton's room, and saw everything. She saw the winning trophies of Morton's which he got from his dance competition. She opens the wardrobe, it's full of Aariana's romantic poems. Morton breaks all the gifts of Aariana but not her love and romantic poems, Which he likes most.She reads all the poems of Aariana.

She sits in his bed and sees all the materials which are on his table. She can find the diary of Morton. He writes all about Aariana's and their loves , sexual relationships, Pains and breakups. She turns over the pages one by one. After some pages he didn't write anything. After some pages she can find some images and drawings which are similar to her room's weird paintings.She can feel something wrong. So, She continued the pages and reached the last page.She can find the quote which is shocking to her.

" My love doesn't want to hurt you, But it gives endless support to you...."

These are the quotes of Ransley.

Next morning, Cassandra went to Joshua's home with Morton's diary. She explains,

Cassandra with a shocking excited voice : " Joshua, see these pictures can you remember?"

Joshua thinks and he got remembered,

Joshua : " This is the picture , I have seen in your wardrobe. The same weird image."

Cassandra : " Yes, And see these quotes." Cassandra shows Ransley's quotes and explains about those quotes.

" This quote was written by Ransley for me and my love" Says Cassandra.

Joshua : " Then something happened, I have a doubt with Abaddon and your Father Miller."

Cassandra : " Come to my Father's office , Will ask about this?"

Joshua : " No, If Abaddon involves this means, That's dangerous for our life. Will go to Bran's home and inform him."

Both Joshua and Cassandra went to Bran's home and told him about what they had discussed and Cassandra showed the diary to him and She explained about those quotes.

Bran is already aware of those quotes, Which he saw in Ransley's home while investigating his mother. He confirmed that Miller was involved in this case. Bran makes ready and gets the enquired letter officially.

Bran came to Miller's office and asked Miller to come enquiry officially about Ransley's death.

Miller : " Bran, Don't do stupid things. You have already seen in murder place what was happened really to Ransley. Then, why do you want to investigate me."

Bran : "No Miller, I can't believe that. Frankly, I have doubt with you about Ransley's death and your son Morton's death."

Miller : "You are spoiling my business career. How much do you get from my opponent's business company?"

Bran : " I am not a businessman like you, This is an official letter. You have to come with me."

Finally, Miller went to Bran for investigation.

Bran wants to know at least a single clue. So he decided to give drugs to Miller and get the information from his subconscious mind.

In the investigation room, Bran wants to take the video recorder of Miller's statement.And he starts asking questions.

Bran : " Why did you kill Ransley and your son?"

Miller : " What the fuck you are talking," He is taking breathe and say , " Sorry Bran, Why should I have to kill Morton, and spoil my good names."

Bran : " You killed your son to keep your good name."

Miller :" Sorry, I can't understand."

Bran stands and walks over the room and stands behind Miller, He keeps drugs in his injection and makes it ready, Paralelly he is explaining also.

Bran : " After my phone call you know about Morton's and Ransley's fight. After that you had discussed with your son about that. He agreed with your words. So,to keep your good name, you have killed your son and inform us like a suicide right?"

Miller : " No, It's disgusting. If you want to ask my daughter."

Unexpectedly, he injects the drugs to the back neck of Miller.

Miller : " What the fuck are you doing. You asshole it's paining. I will kill you.." His voice slows down quietly. Now Miller is half conscious and Bran asks questions about Ransley's death and his doubts.

Miller telling about Ransley's murder, Abaddon planning, Morton's love failure, Claudia's brain death, Ransley's soul transformation, Murder place incident planning with Bran, Aariana death, and Morton's death.

Bran gets shocked and he's sweaty.. He took some water and documented everything and the video camera also recorded the same.

Every word is heard by Cassandra and Joshua from the next of the investigation room through microphone and speaker. Cassandra cries uncontrollably. Joshua in shock and speechless.

Bran asked about Abaddon availability now. But he doesn't know about him.

The Sinland government gives life sentence punishment to Miller. And Death penalty to Abaddon. Miller is inside the prison. He is worrying about his sin. Cassandra and Joshua are married together and live peacefully with lots of love. Cassandra takes over the company of Steve Miller leathers. Bran and his department search Aabaddon in the entire Sinland city. Bran is thinking about Ransley's soul. While examining the Abaddon place. He can't find any mirror like the words of Joshua.

One fine day, Police caught Abaddon's dead body inside the sinland hill forest. They removed his black glasses and saw his eyes. His one eye is brown in color like a cat, and another eye is blue in color. Bran went to the forest and saw Aabadon's face. After 5 minutes, Bran got the news from prison, Miller gets suicide by pluck out his throut by himself. Bran got shocked and he went there. Miller already donates his body organs to sinland hospital. So, after official formalities , In front of Joshua and Cassandra , They had completed the funeral of Miller's and Abaddon's body.

Bran is able to guess the mysteries and he knows, **" This is not going to end"**.
The Play:

After bran afraid and left from Ransley's murder place. Abaddon thinks lonely and deeply in his place.Abaddon has planned to take the shares of Steve Miller Leathers from all successful projects.So,He used Ransley's soul. Abaddon injects his own evilness to Ransley's soul. Abaddon has a sexual attraction with womens especially Cassandra. He wants to make a sex with Cassandra from her schooling days. So, that same evilness is behaved by Ransley's soul through Morton. Abaddon murder Ransley's mother and lock her soul into his mirror. Whatever they are dealing with in Ransley's soul are the words of Abaddon. Abaddon takes the shares of Miller Industries profits by the name of Ransley's mother. Miller isn't aware of this plan. Unfortunately, Miller kills Morton, So abaddon gets angry with Miller and he decides to make another plan. Again he took the control of Ransley , Claudia, Ransley's mother, Aariana's souls and he locked into a glass pot and he was buried out into the earth. After some days, He went to the hill forest and he separated his soul from his own body and entered into Miller's body. He influenced Miller's soul to kill himself.

Days passed on…………….

Present day,

One fine night, Cassandra is having sex with Joshua in her naked body. Joshua pulled Cassendra into down and he's is fucking Cassandra. His face is behind her neck. Cassandra closes her eyes and moans. Slowly, Joshua's eyes are turned into Brown and Blue.

Yes, Abaddon's soul has entered into Joshua's body....Rest is imaginary….

Following negative ways and negative power will not only affect the respective person. But also their family and their future too.

www.ingramcontent.com/pod-product-compliance
Lightning Source LLC
Chambersburg PA
CBHW081301130726
47998CB00010B/2884